≠
Sm51b

BILLY BOONE

ALISON SMITH

CHARLES SCRIBNER'S SONS
NEW YORK

Charles Scribner's Sons Books for Young Readers
Macmillan Publishing Company
866 Third Avenue, New York, NY 10022
Collier Macmillan Canada, Inc.

Printed in the United States of America
First Edition   10 9 8 7 6 5 4 3 2 1

Library of Congress Cataloging-in-Publication Data
Smith, Alison, date.   Billy Boone.
Summary: Twelve-year-old Billy fights for her right to take trumpet lessons and spend time with her unorthodox grandmother, even though her parents believe these activities will not help her grow up in a ladylike fashion.
    [1. Sex role—Fiction.   2. Trumpet—Fiction.   3. Musician—Fiction.   4. Grandmothers—Fiction]   I. Title.
    PZ7.S6425Bi   1989   [Fic]   88–34839
                ISBN 0–684–18974–7

TO EVAN "DOC" SMITH

who taught me everything I know

about the trumpet

BILLY BOONE

1

None of this would have happened if I'd been born a boy.

Actually, my father was expecting a boy . . . but my mother was expecting a girl.

My father likes girls all right, but by the time I came, he'd already *had* two of them. He'd been saving his father's name—William C. Boone—for a son. When I arrived, he gave up on getting a "William" and called me "Billy." (My brother William, who arrived four years later, was a real surprise.)

When I was about five, my grandmother on my father's side, Joy Cometh In The Morning (that's from the Bible) Boone, arrived in our town, to stay. The family called her Joy for short till she grew up and made them all call her Dixie instead. She brought a genuine Appalachian dulcimer, a Confederate rifle in working condition, and a big, old hound dog named Beagle (because he wasn't).

She was supposed to move in with us, but my mother, who is very practical, drew the line at Beagle and the rifle, and Dixie drew the line at giving them up, so my father found Dixie a little place down the road, and the shouting stopped. But even though no one was yelling any longer, things were not exactly all grits and gravy.

For one thing, my mother thought that Dixie swore too much, too often. For another, she felt that Dixie should spend more time on constructive things like housework and meeting people. Dixie did a lot of reading, and she loved the game shows on TV. She'd answer all the questions and cuss out the emcee and encourage the contestants at the top of her lungs. When her eyes were tired, she'd sit outside on her porch and do what she called "keeping an eye on the neighborhood." When I was younger, I figured this made her sort of an auxiliary policeman, and I felt safer just knowing that my grandmother was doing it.

To tell you the truth, Dixie took some getting used to. She didn't care what anyone else said, and she would just tell you in a minute exactly what *she* thought. This meant that she didn't have many friends, because people don't really like to get news like that, hot off the griddle. I, myself, didn't go to see her very often at first. When one of the others went down to her place, I'd say, "My stomach doesn't feel well," or "I think I'm getting a terrible cold." But then, after a few upset stomachs and terrible colds that never really amounted to much, my father began to say, "Billy, darling, I'll just bet your granny's wondering when you're going to go see her again," which meant "It's your turn, Billy—get going." My mother, who thought Dixie was a bad influence, would sniff and slam pots around for a while, and I'd go, just to get out of the cross fire.

Another thing that scared me a little was that rifle. It hung on the wall, right over her fireplace, and whenever I sat on the sofa, I could just see it falling off its hooks and hitting the floor and going off, straight into my heart. My mother always said that someday it *would* go off and kill someone, and I didn't want that someone to be me.

When I'd known Dixie for about three years, I told her how scared I was of that rifle, and she took it down and showed me that it wasn't loaded and let me help her clean it.

After that, I started going down to see her every chance I got, on my own, and the better I knew her, the more I liked her. If I'd been a boy, I'd probably have tagged along behind my father all the time, or Uncle Joe, who plays poker and shoots pool better than anyone else in town, when he can find someone to play with him, and who smokes big cigars and has a gorgeous, curly black mustache that goes clear from one side of his face to the other. But I didn't figure they'd want a girl tagging along behind them, so I just naturally ended up spending a lot of time with Dixie. My mother works three days a week, and when she's home, she's really, really busy. Dixie is never busy.

Anyhow, last summer, when I turned twelve, three things happened—Bing. BANG! BOOM!!!—that changed Dixie and me forever.

The first was a convention of people who play with tin soldiers. They got together and set up their soldiers and their forts on big tables laid out like battlefields, with little fake trees and hills and roads, and then they fought famous battles all over again. Dixie and I were out shopping, and she wanted to sit down somewhere cool to rest her feet, without having to pay for the privilege, so we sat in the lobby of the Hotel Fontainebleu, in the center of town, and tried to look as if we were waiting for someone who was staying at the hotel.

Right in the middle of the lobby, these grown-ups had set up a big display of their toys. I think it was the battle of Waterloo, but I'm not sure. I was concentrating on the bellhop, who was real cute and a junior at our high school.

Dixie got up, walked around the table, and asked a fellow standing beside the display what it was all about—and that did it! Half an hour later, we were down at Schwartz's Sporting Goods, Toys Also, buying Schwartz out. Dixie had me hung with little packages like a Christmas tree by the time we left. Tiny soldiers and guns and horses and equipment—

all from the Civil War. She spent her whole Social Security check, and she and Beagle had to eat beans for a month.

She set up her battlegrounds on her kitchen table for a while, but it was too small. Her troops kept falling off. Some got broken, and one of the fake trees disappeared. We *think* Beagle ate it, because he had indigestion for several days afterward and had to be kept outside. So Dixie told my father she thought she should move her forces up to our house and use the Ping-Pong table in the basement, which we never used anyway. And my father, without asking my mother, which even *I* could have told him was a big mistake, said, "Sure, Ma—whatever makes you happy."

Dixie had a big battle set up down there before my mother got home from work that day, and she'd talked me and my sisters into helping her. Cornelia, who's eighteen, and Melissa, who's sixteen, were supposed to move the Union troops. Dixie and I were in charge of the Confederates. I can't remember what battle it was, but I do remember that the Union was supposed to have won it. Back then. Not now. Dixie figured out how the Confederates should have fought that battle to win, and *that's* how we played it.

From then on, that's how we played every battle. The South won every time. I didn't care. I just did what Dixie told me. Besides, that meant I was always on the winning side. But Cornelia and Melissa felt that we should stick to the facts, and when William, who's only eight, had to fill in for one of us, he, having been born in the North, resented seeing his side get whipped every single time. These "war games," as my father called them, got to be pretty exciting, with everyone standing around arguing and then stomping off upstairs, mad, and then coming back down again.

My mother would never even go down to the basement anymore except to put clothes in the washer. We knew better than to ask her to move Grant's men around. When my mother ignores something and won't even admit it's there and sets her lips like a sealed envelope—watch out!

The second thing was the Fourth of July parade. I love parades. Melissa and Cornelia are too grown-up for parades, they think, and William, being so cute and all—with red hair and freckles and chubby cheeks—always ends up cruising down Main Street on someone's float instead of standing on the sidewalk sweating with the rest of us. My mother and father had a golf date, so it was just Dixie and I watching the parade go by.

The best part of any parade, for me, is the bands. Boy, do I love to hear a band coming toward me and see the sun flashing off the brass instruments and feel the beat of the drums coming up through the hot soles of my feet. The hair goes up on my arms, and I tingle all over.

I said, "I wish I were in a band," and Dixie said,

"Honey, I'll bet you'd be terrific!" and I said, "Yeah. But I'd want to play the trumpet." I was looking right at the band as it marched by and—believe me—not one trumpet player was a girl. There were a couple of girls playing other instruments, but everyone in the trumpet section was a boy.

But Dixie said, "Well, Why not?" as if boy/girl didn't even matter, and that was the second big thing, because right then I began to ask myself, over and over, Why not? It stuck in my mind. Every time I thought about it, I'd get that same tingle. Me—marching down Main Street in a green-and-white uniform with gold trim, and my trumpet glittering in the sun and the notes coming out of it ringing high and clear in the air from one end of the town to the other. If I thought about it for more than a minute, I had to get up. I couldn't stay down. It was *that* exciting to me. I decided that, come fall, I would join the school band and learn to play the trumpet.

The third thing was that I grew. Lord—how I grew! My mother is a small person, with a waist my father can put his hands around. My father is a big man and not thin. You could call him comfortable. He says that he's spreading out around his middle to make up for what he's losing on top, meaning his hair. He has to let his belt out after dinner, usually, and he's getting a double chin.

Anyhow, Cornelia's small and dark and cute, and Melissa's small and dark and cute, and up until I was twelve, I'd kind of hoped I'd end up small and dark

7

and cuter than either of them. But sometime around the end of July, when I passed both of them and kept on going, I knew I was going to end up like my father. My father's just about the nicest father in the world, but I didn't really want to look like him—not as long as I was a girl. And when I heard that each generation now is getting taller than the last one, I knew I was *doomed,* because he's six foot two. If I end up taller than that, I will just die.

I'd always been an outdoors type—swimming, hiking, riding my bicycle, helping my father in the yard—and I wondered if maybe that had set me off and made me tall, but Dixie said, "No. Your grandfather was tall, and his father before him. It's all hereditary anyway, so why not just stand up straight and enjoy it?" Which is fine for Dixie to say, she being small and not caring what anyone else thinks anyway. But next year there will be dances at school from seven to nine in the evening, and what boy is going to dance with a girl who can look down on the part in his hair? I decided that I would just concentrate on the trumpet and forget about boys altogether.

I guess it was the middle of August when the feathers hit the fan. We'd had a long spell of hot, sticky weather, with everyone getting more edgy by the minute. Dixie and I had spent the day on her front porch, sipping lemonade and doing crossword puzzles, and telling each other how hot it was and what we'd give for a good old "the power's out and Main Street's flooded" thunderstorm. When it got to be about four o'clock, Dixie roused herself and said, "Come on, Billy. If I sit here another minute, I'll stick to the chair. Let's go up to the big house"—she always said that, as if our place were the old plantation on the hill—"and give Ulysses S. Grant a chance to redeem his honor."

Well, with Dixie calling the shots, I didn't see much chance of Grant winning, but it would be better than sitting there itching while the sweat ran down my neck. So I nodded and got up.

We'd been setting up, getting everyone into position, for about half an hour, when Cornelia and Melissa came down to watch because it was cooler in the basement. Then William and two of his smart-mouthed friends came down and pulled out some bar stools and sat down. Then my father came home and brought his can of beer down with him. So by the time we started attacking and counterattacking, the basement was full of people.

Naturally, right away Dixie started setting things up for a Southern victory, and right away Melissa and Cornelia crowded around and told her she was going about it all wrong. William and his friends wanted to bring in some Indians—Indians, for corn's sake!—and my father noticed that one of the table legs was getting wobbly.

I don't know how it happened. My father had crawled under the table and taken his shoe off and

9

started pounding on something with it. I was stretched out over the table, getting some Confederate troops out of a jam they'd gotten themselves into. William's friends were running around the table, yelling that the wagons should form a circle, bumping into us and each other, and giving out Indian war whoops, when all of a sudden, for no reason, the table collapsed and the whole battlefield—troops, horses, and all—came sliding down onto the floor and around the feet of Cornelia, Melissa, and Dixie.

My father shouted and swore, Cornelia and Melissa screamed, William and his friends started laughing like hyenas, and Dixie started fussing at everybody because she was worried about her troops and equipment. I was trying to pull my father out from under the table when my mother's voice cut right through all that noise like a hot knife through butter. She was mad. Boy, was she mad!

She stood there on the cellar steps and let everyone have it, starting with my father and ending with Dixie. She was mad about the dining-room table not being set or the dinner started (that would be Cornelia and Melissa, mostly), she was mad about the Ping-Pong table being split, she was mad about my father maybe getting hurt, but most of all, she was mad at Dixie. She told Dixie she was wasting her time and everyone else's playing childish games. She said she was sick and tired of hearing a fuss and commotion coming up from the basement, day after day, and the kids neglecting their chores. She said she wanted every bit of Dixie's war-games stuff out of that basement in twenty-four hours.

Then it was Dixie's turn. I waited, holding my breath. Everyone looked at her, because we knew what Dixie could do when she got angry enough. And she was angry now. She stood there as straight and stiff as a poker. She looked right at my mother for what felt like an hour and never said one word. Then she bent down and started packing her things into their boxes.

For just a moment or two, we all stood there. Then my father made a little movement with his hand, and Cornelia and Melissa shot upstairs to work on setting the table and starting dinner. William's friends mumbled to William and slid past my mother as if they were glad to get out of there alive. I stayed to help Dixie.

My father said, "I'll do that, Billy," but I said, "No!" and kept on working. So he headed for the stairs. As he reached her step, my mother turned and went on up ahead of him. William hung around for a minute, and then he left, too.

It must have been seven o'clock before we had everything packed up to suit Dixie. During all that time, she never said anything to me except "Pass me that box, would you, Billy?" and "Here—this is what you're looking for." When we were through, she asked me if I thought we could borrow William's old express wagon, and I said sure—it was

11

under the basement stairs. So we piled almost everything into the wagon, and tied the boxes down with string, and carried the wagon upstairs and out the front door.

It was a little embarrassing, pulling a kid's red wagon down the street, but I didn't want Dixie to be embarrassed alone. When we got to her house, I helped her unload the wagon. Then she said, "You run along, now, Billy. Your mother will be keeping some dinner for you."

I left. I didn't want to argue with Dixie. But I didn't want to go, either. Her house, behind her as she stood on the front porch, was dark and lonely looking. Old Beagle lay in the doorway, but he wasn't much company. He's the only dog I ever met who could fall asleep while he was waiting for you to finish filling his dinner bowl. He's not lively, if you get my point.

I thought of what it would be like to go into that house, all alone, after being sent packing like that . . . and I almost couldn't keep on walking. I wanted to run back and put my arms around Dixie and hold her tight, but I didn't dare. I didn't dare because I was afraid that if I did, Dixie might break down and cry, and Dixie crying . . . I didn't know how I could bear that. So I just walked on home and didn't even look back once—which shows you what kind of a friend I am.

2

From then on, Dixie kept her troops in her kitchen and never mentioned my mother.

At home, Ma never asked about Dixie. I noticed, though, that whenever I said, "Well, I guess I'll just go on down to Dixie's house this afternoon," Ma would always find something for me to do so I wouldn't be able to go. And if I said *anything*—like, "Couldn't I do that tonight instead, Ma?"—she would really let me have it.

So when I wanted to spend some time with Dixie, I would just sort of glide over what I planned to do. And if Ma tried to pin me down, I'd lie. I'd say, "Oh, Ma, I don't know. Maybe Geraldine is home. We'll just fool around her place." I knew lying wasn't right, but it seemed like the only thing I could do if I wanted to keep on seeing Dixie without stirring up a lot of trouble.

When Dixie asked me why I wasn't coming around so often, I didn't want to tell her right out that Ma was keeping me busy on purpose, so I'd say, "I had a little cold, Dixie. I didn't want you and Beagle to catch it."

It was no big thing, really. The only bit that worried me about it, right then, was what to do if Geraldine called to talk to me while I was supposed to be over at her house. Finally, I quit worrying about that and figured I'd cross that bridge when I got to it.

School started right after Labor Day, and band started right after school. I was ready! When they announced that Beginners' Band would meet the following Monday, I nearly cheered, right out loud, in class. But I restrained myself and turned around and whispered to Geraldine, "I'm going to sign up for the band."

"You are?"

"I'm going to learn the trumpet."

"The trumpet?"

Geraldine is all right, but she has this habit of answering everything you say with a question. It's sort of like conversing with an echo.

"Yes, the trumpet. Why don't you sign up, too?"

"Me? Sign up for the band? But I wouldn't want to play the trumpet."

"Geraldine, you don't *have* to play—"

Mrs. French cut in and said that if Geraldine and I

14

were willing, she'd like to have the class's attention back so that she could proceed with the lesson. So I had to knock it off.

I stopped by Dixie's on the way home from school.

"They're signing up for band next Monday after school. Anyone can join, and they're going to arrange for lessons and renting the instruments and all that for the people who don't play yet."

"And you're going to sign up for the trumpet."

"I sure am."

"Have you told your dad yet?"

"I just heard about it today. I'll tell him tonight."

"He's going to be so pleased. I know he was keenly disappointed when Cornelia and Melissa stopped practicing and quit piano."

"Well, I'm not going to quit the trumpet."

"I know you won't, hon. Beagle, if I fall over you one more time, I'm going to brain you with this skillet, so help me. Now, move it! Will you have a cookie, Billy?"

I hung around for a while, eating cookies and talking, and then I had to go. If I came home too late on a day Ma wasn't working, she'd want to know where I'd been, and then I'd have to lie, or tell her the truth and have her snap my head off all evening.

When I told Dad I was going to sign up for band, he was really pleased. When I said I'd be taking the trumpet, he made a face as if he smelled something unpleasant.

"Now, Billy, honey—can't we find a more suitable instrument for you to play?" Then his face evened out into a big smile. "Hey, darling, we've got one of the best pianos ever made, just sitting there in the front room, and I'll bet that lady who taught your sisters how to play is still around. How about it?"

I couldn't believe what I was hearing. In the first place, who ever saw anyone pushing a Steinway down the street in the middle of a parade? And, in the second place, "that lady" who taught Melissa and Cornelia was one of the main reasons why they quit. She made them play scales by the hour till even Ma had had it—and when she did give them a piece to learn it was always something like "The Daffodil Song." *One*-two-three-four, *one*-two-three-four, "*In* the fields of *Spring* you'll find me, *Un*derneath the *whis*pering trees . . . ," when Melissa and Cornelia were just aching to learn how to play the stuff they were dancing to on Saturday nights. And, in the third place, I don't like the piano. I mean, either you like something or you don't. I *do* like the trumpet. I do *not* like the piano.

So I said, very calmly, "Daddy, I don't want to play the piano."

"But, darling, how can you tell? Till you've tried it, I mean."

"I don't have to get hit by a truck to know I'm not going to like it."

He said, "Billy, don't you sass me!" And my

16

mother came in and said, "If you're going to start yelling at each other, I'm going to go shopping till the stores close, and you can all feed yourselves."

So I took off for my bedroom and left Dad folding his paper as if he were beating it to death.

Monday morning I said to Dad, "Band meets this afternoon."

He started to cut up his pancakes. "Is that a fact?"

"Yes. Are you going to let me take the trumpet or not?"

"Now, Billy, if you go playing something like a trumpet year after year, it'll ruin your pretty mouth. You don't want to do that, do you?"

William said, "Hey, Billy, that's neat. Can I try it out when you bring it home?" And Cornelia said, "Really, Billy, do you have to be such a tomboy all the time? You know you're not going to keep it up. It's just going to be one more thing . . ."

I let Cornelia have it first because she was asking for it. "Listen, Cornelia, you've got a lot of nerve to talk to me like that. You and Melissa quit piano after two years of lessons, so don't you go telling me what to do."

Cornelia started to give me a song and dance about how busy she and Melissa were, but I knew that they always had time for anything they really wanted to do, so I just let her run on.

I told William he could try the trumpet—just once—when I got it.

17

And then I asked Dad, who was halfway through his pancakes by now, what he meant about ruining my mouth.

"Why, I should think it would make your mouth so much bigger, Billy—all that blowing and all. It just stands to reason."

"Well, if I want to anyway, can I?"

"I don't know, Billy."

"I ought to be able to at least try. You bought that piano and paid for lessons for Cornelia and Melissa."

He shoved his pancakes away. "I swear you get more like your grandmother every day."

"Does that mean yes?"

"Yes." But he didn't look happy about it.

"Thanks, Dad." And I gave him a big, fast kiss on the cheek. Not the lips—or someone else would have had to pour hot water over us to separate us, after all that syrup.

Before I left for school, I stood in front of the mirror and looked at my face. Would a bigger mouth make a difference? I couldn't see that it would. No one was ever going to run me for Miss America anyway—so, since I didn't have a gorgeous face, why shouldn't I have a useful face, like, at the small end of a trumpet? I felt a lot better.

The bandleader's name was Helmut Kruger. He was tall, with a big cloud of frizzy, teddy-bear-colored hair around the back and sides of his head; the top and front were shiny bald. He had a German accent, and I'd heard he also had a very short temper. By Christmas vacation, on the wall of the school yard, you would always see "To Hell with Hel," written in ink or lipstick or chalk, where kids who had just had trouble with him had expressed themselves.

The room was crowded with kids. Most of them had instruments, and most of them were boys. Well, I expected that, right? We were all nervous—I more than anybody, I think. It would have been better if I'd already had an instrument. It would have given me something to hang on to, and it would have made me look more as if I belonged.

When Mr. Kruger walked in, everyone straightened up and stopped talking. He went right to the front of the room, without looking around or saying a word.

When he had put his briefcase down and gotten all settled in behind the desk, he looked up.

"You will all form a line over there, and you will approach the desk one at a time. There will be no pushing, no shoving, and no talking."

That was the quietest line I'd ever been in. My hands were sweating and my knees were a little shaky. I found a spot about halfway back, so I wouldn't have to be among the first or live through waiting to be the last.

By the time I was face to face with Mr. Kruger, I was just glad I hadn't eaten anything before I came. But I kept telling myself that it would all be over in a few more minutes, and I hung on.

"Name?"

"Billy—that's with a Y—Boone."

"Instrument?"

"Trumpet."

He looked up at me with a strange expression. "Really? How many years?"

"Not any, yet. I'm just starting. I'd like to start."

"What other instrument do you play?"

"None. We *have* a piano, but I don't like the piano."

He looked up at the ceiling as if something was written up there and he was trying to read it.

"Why do you want to play the trumpet?"

Before I'd thought about it, I said, "Why not?"

He glared at me and said, very slowly, "I beg your pardon?"

"I mean—I just do. I didn't mean to sound fresh, honestly, Mr. Kruger. It's just that Geraldine said, 'The trumpet?' and my father tried to talk me out of it—and I don't see why not."

"The trumpet is a very masculine instrument."

For a minute, he had me stumped. Was that the reason that only boys could play it? Then I pictured what a trumpet looked like. *Anybody* could handle a trumpet. "I don't understand."

"It's an aggressive instrument, Miss. It's a strong instrument. It takes a lot of wind and control."

I nodded. He was so right!

"Still you wish to play the trumpet?"

"Yes, Mr. Kruger."

He handed me the form he'd been filling out. "Take this home. Get your parents to read it and sign it, and bring it back. Without it you will not be allowed to rent an instrument or take a lesson or be in the band. Is that clear?"

"Yes, sir, Mr. Kruger."

"Next."

I could go! I was one big step closer to having a trumpet in my hands.

3

I stopped in at Dixie's on the way home and told her about Mr. Kruger and showed her the form and ate about a dozen cookies. It was pretty late when I left, so when I got home and Ma asked, "Where have you been?" I said, "At Geraldine's," which was the first thing that came into my head.

I always get zapped when I least expect it. I could have told the truth—or at least part of it. Ma must have heard about the band meeting from Dad. But no—I've got to lie, for no good reason. I guess it had gotten to be a habit for me.

"That's not true."

"What do you mean?" I could tell I was in trouble, but I wasn't sure why—or how deep.

"Geraldine called here twice this afternoon, wondering how the band meeting had gone."

"Oh."

"I had a long talk with Geraldine, Billy Boone. You've been lying to me right along, haven't you? When did the meeting end?"

"I left about four."

"It's almost six."

"I stopped in to say hello to Gran'ma and Beagle."

"I knew it! And you lied about it. Does your grandmother know you've been lying about seeing her?"

"No. Of course she doesn't."

"Don't get up on your high horse with me, girl. You're the one who's been caught lying. And we all know your grandmother says what suits her."

Well, Ma was right. I had lied, and Dixie had been known to stretch the truth a little. She didn't exactly lie. She just sort of touched things up. If Beagle caught two rabbits and brought them home, she might lead you to believe he'd rounded up nearly a half-dozen. When it rained so hard that all our basements were flooded, Dixie always had more water in hers than anyone else. My father said she was a great storyteller and one of a vanishing breed. My mother acted like the sooner they vanished, the better. It seemed as if the wilder Dixie's stories got, the more careful to be accurate my mother got, till you'd swear she carried a tape measure around with her. They just seemed to make each other worse.

Ma said, "Go to your room and stay there."

I went. Sometimes I argue a little, but tonight I knew I'd better not, if I wanted to live.

Dad got home a few minutes later. I could hear him coming in. He put his briefcase down too close to the edge of that little table in the front hall, and it fell off and took the table with it. Dad is not a quiet person. He bangs into things and knocks things over and drops things, without ever meaning to. Dixie says it's because he's such a magnificent, big man, and she's probably right. He is big, all right.

For a long time after Dad and Ma had straightened up the front hall, they talked about me in the living room. I could hear the voices going up and down, and once I heard Ma really hitting the high notes. Dad never does yell. The most he will do is mutter loudly, as if he were growling the words up through his throat. If you're the one he's growling at, that can be more scary than a shout, because he doesn't do it very often.

Cornelia came home and left the door to the living room wide open, and suddenly I could hear every word.

"All summer long, she was never around when there was work for her to do. All I had to do was open the cleaning cabinet and she was gone, and I wouldn't see her for the rest of the day. Sometimes I wouldn't see her except for meals twice a day, for a week at a time. Now, that isn't healthy—sitting in that dark little house, all day long, watching TV."

"Well, I'll certainly speak to her about that. She should help out around the place."

"And someday, you mark my words, that rifle is

24

going to go off and take someone's head off. I don't want it to be Billy's."

"Barbara, honey, the rifle isn't loaded. Ma wouldn't hang it up there ready to fire. You know she wouldn't."

"And another thing, Charles. No offense, but the last time I was down there, there was a row of empty whiskey bottles as long as my arm, on a table in the backyard. Lined up for target practice, no doubt. I didn't want to say anything about it, but you ought to speak to Dixie. It'll get to her liver, if it hasn't already."

"I believe those are old bottles—sort of collector's items, you might say. She only sips a little bourbon, to mark special occasions."

"I'll bet! And she coughs. Constantly. She never smoked in her life, but she's always coughing. I do believe she has TB. And Billy's down there all the time, being exposed."

"Now, that's ridiculous. Ma's probably healthier than either one of us. You're going way overboard, Barbara."

"She's a bad influence, Charles. She swears, terribly—and she has no respect for the truth—and she cannot stand me. She looks down on me, Charles. I can see it—just as clear—every time I'm down there."

"Barbara, honey, how could anyone look down on you? You're just about the smartest, prettiest little woman—"

"Oh, Charles, for heaven's sake! You never notice that kind of thing anyway. She'd have to hit me over the head with a club and come and tell you about it before you'd think anything was wrong."

One of them must have realized that the door was open, because I heard it shut—hard—and from then on, all I could hear was a confused murmur. They were at it so long, I began to get a little scared.

4

They called me in, finally. Oh, boy—it was going to be two against one.

"Yes, Dad?" I figured he was my only hope. Ma looked as if she was still mad enough to disown me.

"Now, Billy, I said you—"

"Reluctantly," my mother said, cutting in. "You were reluctant."

"I was reluctant," my father said, turning his whole body away from me to face her, "but I did give my word, and that's that. I said Billy could take trumpet."

I took in a deep breath. So—he wasn't going to let me down and go back on his word.

He turned back to me. "However, we just cannot tolerate your deceiving your mother. No, sir. That's something we have never allowed our children to do."

27

"I'm sorry. I just didn't know what else to do, Dad. If I saw Gran'ma and said I had, Ma didn't like it. If I saw Gran'ma and didn't say I had, no one was upset."

My mother said, "You have overlooked a third possibility that apparently never even occurred to you."

"Yes, Ma'am?"

"Seeing your grandmother only on those occasions when we felt it was a good idea . . . which would mean not having to lie and not upsetting anyone."

"But Dixie needs me . . . she gets lonely."

"She doesn't have to get lonely," my mother said. "She is free to come and go as she wishes. There are dozens of activities for people her age every month at the senior citizens' center in town."

"Dixie says they treat you like you need help going to the bathroom, down there."

"She would say that, of course. Nothing is ever good enough, unless it involves everyone crowding around her and granting her every wish. She will go to any length to be the center of attention. . . . That rifle, for instance."

By now, I could see that my mother was working up a full head of steam again. My father glanced at her as if he was getting up a pretty good head of steam himself. My stomach tied itself into a knot.

"That's neither here nor there, is it, Barbara? Why

28

don't you just tell Billy about the piano and let it go at that?"

A cold shiver ran up and down my spine. Piano? Piano? What had they cooked up for me now that had something to do with the piano? My mother cleared her throat and breathed carefully for a moment or two. She hyperventilates sometimes, if she isn't careful, and has to sit down with a brown paper bag up to her face for a few minutes till she feels better.

"To make a long story short, Billy, you will also be required to take piano, a more suitable instrument in every way. It is *the* basic instrument, after all. Everything you learn on it will help you with every other instrument—even the trumpet."

She said "even the trumpet" as if the trumpet were some kind of disease.

"Mrs. Ramsbottom will be happy to take over your musical education, and our piano—which is one of the best money can buy—will be serving some purpose, instead of just sitting there taking up space and constantly needing dusting."

Boy, I thought, this is going to be some musical year, with trumpet instruction Mondays and band rehearsal Thursdays and practice at home on the trumpet all the other days, plus a lesson once a week with Mrs. Ramsbottom. I'd be up to my ears in scales and songs and all the rest of it. And if I actually practiced the piano—plus taking the lessons— I'd be busy all afternoon, every afternoon.

Then it hit me. That was it! I'd be busy every day—too busy to visit Dixie and too busy even to talk on the phone with Geraldine. I was being railroaded! By my own mother.

I said, very politely, "It is a good piano, but I do not wish to play the piano."

My mother said, "How many adult women do you know who play the trumpet, compared with those who still keep up with the piano? And no one can tell whether she'll like a thing or not till she's tried it."

I toyed with the idea of using the getting-hit-by-a-truck bit, but when I caught my father's eye, I knew he realized what I was thinking and he was signaling me not to try it. I kept my mouth shut. This was one of those days when my mother wasn't taking anything from anybody.

So—that was that. I was doomed to the piano till Ma cooled down or Dad took pity on me or they both got so sick of "The Daffodil Song" that they couldn't take it any longer.

I wanted to go right down and fill Dixie in on the whole situation, but of course that was out. Dixie and Beagle would have to get along without me for a while. It was going to be tough on them, but I thought they could handle it. The part that was even tougher was that I was going to have to get along without them for a while. When I thought about that, I could have cried very easily. It'd gotten so that every time I had good news or bad news or just a question in my mind, my first idea was to go right down and talk it over with Dixie. Not seeing her, except maybe on Sunday afternoons—dull, DULL, DULL—would make a big difference to me every single day.

I did call her on the phone in the kitchen, when everyone was busy somewhere else, and tell her that I had been caught telling a lie to Ma and had been sentenced to the piano—and what with the trumpet and the band *and* the piano, I was going to be all tied up for a long time. There were long, silent times during the conversation when Dixie was probably thinking over what I'd said, or I was trying to find the right way to say something so Dixie wouldn't catch on and get her feelings hurt. It was the first careful talk we'd had with each other in a couple of years. Usually, we just opened up and sprayed it all out.

The piano tuner came and made sure that every note I played would be right on the button. Mrs. Ramsbottom said she would be delighted to add me to her Saturday-morning schedule. Saturday morning! There went a perfectly good day—right down the drain. And the day for collecting my rental trumpet and having my first lesson came closer. It was a good thing I had *something* to look forward to, because I missed Dixie and Beagle.

We were actually going to get our trumpets—and have our first group lesson—on a Monday afternoon. That whole day went by a minute at a time—

9:10, 9:11, 9:12. When the right bell finally rang, I was already exhausted.

About ten of us collected in 116—which is the Small Music Room. Nine boys and me. No Mr. Kruger.

One of the boys—short, fat, red hair and a smart mouth—said, "This class is for trumpets only."

I said, "I know that."

Whereupon they all stopped talking and turned around to give me the once-over.

For just a minute, there, it bothered me. Then I thought, Who are they kidding, Billy Boone? Where is it written that only short, stuck-up boys can blow into a trumpet? You're as good as they are, any day of the week. And I just casually sauntered over to the cases on the table and touched one of them, as though I was trying to decide if this was the one I would allow myself to take.

"You're not supposed to do that," said a tall, stringy-looking one in the back.

"Why not? I'm not hurting anything."

Another person might have been embarrassed. I mean, by now, they were lined up like birds on a telephone wire, looking at me as if I were the neighborhood cat. At times like this, Dixie used to say, a person needs lots of aplomb. I think that means not letting it get to you.

Another thing Dixie says a lot, when she's playing Civil War, is "A good offense is the best defense," which means "Don't stand around waiting to get a pie in the face. Pick up a pie, yourself, first." So, I said to the stringy-looking one, "Are *you* going to play the trumpet?" as if it were just beyond belief that he should do so.

He mumbled something and turned red. The others sort of stirred and changed places.

It was a relief when the door flew open and Mr. Kruger came in. "Ah, good. My new trumpet section. You will line up, over there, and we will see about these instruments."

Ten people don't make for a very long line, so I didn't mind being at the end. There were at least fifteen cases on the table, and I knew Mr. Kruger wouldn't run out of instruments. But I did think that real gentlemen wouldn't have used their elbows the way these clowns did.

Mr. Kruger would snap open a case, look inside to see if there really was a trumpet in there, look at the boy in front of the table, and say, "Name?"

I could see right away that he didn't like mumblers. Maybe it discouraged him to find mumblers in his trumpet section because it is true that you need a lot of wind to blow a horn.

When he found a person's name on his list, he'd make a kind of sad, clucking sound, as if none of us was measuring up, and then he'd say, "Card?" and you were supposed to hand him your permission card. It made him irritable if you dropped it or just laid it down as if you were tired.

33

So when he got to me, and said, "Name?" I said, "Billy Boone, sir," good and loud.

He looked up and nodded. He found my name on his list.

"You have thought over what I said, Billy Boone?"

"Yes, sir." Good and loud.

He sighed. "You have your card?"

"Yes, sir, Mr. Kruger," and I laid it on his outstretched hand so you could hear it hit.

"Thank you." He put it with the others.

He had us all sit down, and then for an hour he talked about the trumpet, how it worked, famous trumpeters he had known, and what kind of behavior he expected at band rehearsal—meaning, absolutely perfect. Then he took his own trumpet out of its gorgeous, velvet-lined case and put it to his lips and played.

Wow! The room was full of trumpet! My ears pinged. I *loved* it. I couldn't wait to put my own trumpet up to my lips and let her rip. It didn't even bother me that he called on me to try it first. I was glad.

That's why it was such a shock when no sound came out. At all. I was blowing in at one end, but nothing was coming out at the other.

I stopped blowing and turned the trumpet around, to see if anything was stuck in the other end. There was no point in my blowing my brains out if there was nowhere for the air to go. Nothing! I shook it and tried again. A little hoarse squeak. By now, of course, the boys were giggling. They were trying to hide it—not because they didn't want to upset me, but because they were scared to death of Mr. Kruger.

I stopped blowing and gave them a look. Mr. Kruger said, "Next," and pointed to the boy in front of me. Period. Not a word of explanation. How was I ever going to learn if he didn't tell me what I was doing wrong? I stood there for a moment, wondering what to do. The kid in front of me stood up, put his horn up to his mouth, and let go.

The last time I heard a noise like that, I had just stepped on one of William's old rubber squeeze-toys. I couldn't help it—I burst out laughing. I guess I was so relieved that someone else was having trouble, too, that I couldn't keep it down. I tried—but all that did was make my laughing sound like a lot of small explosions.

Mr. Kruger hit the desk with a ruler, several times, hard. All of a sudden, I found it real easy to stop laughing.

"Miss Boone, no one laughed when you were playing for us."

"No, sir. I'm sorry."

"See that it does not happen again."

"Yes, sir."

He said, "Next!" and pointed to the short, fat kid.

Well, none of us was any good. By the time I got to go home, my cheeks were tired, my lips ached, and my sides hurt from not laughing. We were all terrible—which was good news for me. If the rest of them had sounded like Mr. Kruger right away, I would have been discouraged.

The Beginners' Band rehearsal on Thursday was scheduled for a regular morning class period. I guess it's considered culture. Then, after school, unless the field was actually under water from heavy rain, there was a Full Band rehearsal, with marching and all. Mr. Kruger said we would not be allowed to attend the marching sessions till we sounded like something on Thursday mornings, so we wouldn't throw the rest of the band off. I think talk like that is what made Mr. Kruger's bands such hot stuff. If you worked morning, noon, and night; if you had lots of talent; if you attended every rehearsal, no matter what; if Mr. Kruger needed you, you might, finally, be allowed to attend the big rehearsals. If you were good enough to meet Mr. Kruger's standards at the big rehearsals, you might possibly be allowed to play in parades and at games and in concerts. Maybe. It got to be a big thing to be in the Tri-Town Marching Band. Ordinarily, I would not care to become involved in a rat race like that. But if it meant learning to play the trumpet with a really good band, I could handle it.

When I walked in Thursday morning, the room was already jammed. The other trumpeters were there—and dozens of other kids, all hanging on to new or rented instruments.

Mr. Kruger walked in and rapped on the podium for attention. "Trumpets over there. Drums up here. French horns there . . ." and so on, till we were all in little clots, divided up by instrument.

"Sit!"

We sat.

"Now I will pass among you, handing out the appropriate music. You will take it, you will hold on to it, and you will remain silent."

The hour went by very rapidly. For us. But not for Mr. Kruger, I think. He lost his temper about once every five minutes and yelled at us in German. About halfway through, he sent one of the drummers out for a cup of water and took a big, white pill. For the last ten minutes or so, he made us stop trying to play and had us just sit there quietly, studying the music.

Naturally, we were not invited to attend the afternoon rehearsal.

Saturday morning I had to get up even earlier than on a school day, just so Mrs. Ramsbottom could fit me in at eight. On the way over, my mother told me how lucky I was; Mrs. Ramsbottom's Saturday schedule was full all the time. Fortunately, she said, someone had canceled for Saturday morning just before Ma had called, and I had gotten that spot. If I ever meet the kid who canceled—Doreen Turkle— I'm going to tell her just exactly what she did to me.

Mrs. Ramsbottom is small and chubby, with

short, curly, gray hair. She wears flowered dresses and high heels all year. Every June she makes all the kids who take lessons from her play in a recital, but I had already promised myself that I was not going to play in any recital. If Ma and Dad put the pressure on, I would just get sick that day, even if it meant sticking a toothbrush down my throat till I threw up. Just thinking about a piano recital made my hands sweaty.

Anyway, we pulled up in front of Mrs. Ramsbottom's house, with those ugly plaster dwarfs hiding in the shrubs and a gross little plaster boy kissing a gross little plaster girl out in front, on the lawn.

I said, "Yuck!"

My mother said, "You're not going to give her trouble, are you, Billy? Because if you are . . ."

Which was very unfair. Not only do I have to take these lessons—which I do not want to take—but I have to be polite and act happy about it. When someone makes my mother do something she doesn't want to do, she may be polite, because she's a lady, but she sure isn't smiling.

I didn't answer. Let a doubt linger in her mind . . . all morning.

Well, as soon as I was seated at the piano, Mrs. Ramsbottom asked to see my hands. She checked them all over for dirt under the nails and food around the fingers. I was so humiliated. Then she told me to spread my hands out wide to see how much stretch I had. Tut-tut! Not enough! For a moment, I wondered if I was going to be excused from piano because of short, stubby fingers and no stretch—but no way! *She* had an exercise for me that would fix all that, provided I did it twice a day, for five minutes, for about sixty years. By now, actually playing the piano was beginning to look good to me. I'd had it with hands.

She gave me five scale exercises to practice all week and one song, "Smiling Flowers," that was absolutely sickening. Even when *she* played it, and hit all the notes right the first time, it was sickening. I was feeling very depressed by the time Ma came for me.

When Ma asked me how everything went, on the way home, I just grunted. I figured if she cared how I felt, she wouldn't make me do this anyway.

Sunday we were all supposed to go over to Dixie's in the afternoon. I don't know whose idea that was, but it sure wasn't Dixie's. She's the "drop-in" type, where you sit around in your old clothes and never mind the clutter or the dust, and sip iced tea or coffee and munch on store-bought cookies, the kind with lots of filling and maybe even a puffy frosting on top. Dixie is a junk-food junkie. So am I. Wholesome things make me sick. I eat them because I don't want my bones to break or my teeth to rot, but they're not my idea of great food.

When we were all ready to go, Ma said, "Billy, you go change this minute," and they all had to sit out in the car and sweat while I took off a nice, soft pair of old jeans and a really cute T-shirt and put on a white nylon dress with lace panels that scratched my skin.

By the time I got into the car, I was feeling itchy and irritable, and everyone was mad at me.

On the way down, I wondered which way Dixie would go. Would she have Beagle lying on top of the old newspapers on the sofa, or would he be shut up in the bedroom? And, knowing how my mother felt about that rifle, would it be hanging on the wall, or in a drawer somewhere? It seemed to me that Beagle and the rifle would be out of sight. Dixie was smart, and she wouldn't want to rile my mother any more than was necessary. If she did, she might not get to see any of us again, ever.

Dixie was wearing an ironed shirt and a very pretty sort of square-dancing skirt. She looked terrific. She said, "Hello," and kind of ducked her head at my mother and Cornelia and Melissa, and she punched William lightly, and she hugged me very hard, and fast, and let me go. My father was the last one in. She smiled up at him.

"I'm real pleased to see you, Charles," she said. "I began to think maybe you'd moved."

My father said, "Now, Ma . . ." but Dixie interrupted him. "Won't you all have a bite to eat? I made some cookies, and there's iced tea in the pitcher."

I almost fell over. Dixie—making cookies? Where were the bags of Toodle Puffs, with the marsh-

40

mallow coconut frosting, and the Chock-O-Locks, with about half an inch of chocolate filling? These homemade jobs were thin, dry, and about as filling as a brown lace doily.

Beagle and the rifle were nowhere to be seen, but every so often, from way in the back of the house, I could hear a sad, sad howl—as if someone had just died. It kind of stopped conversation whenever it drifted by. Beagle was not used to being shut away from Dixie.

We all sat around—perched—as if we would be taking off in a minute. Everyone tried to talk, but the conversation went in spurts, with long, dead spaces in between. My head began to ache. Dixie looked very unhappy. The only person who didn't look as if he were in a dentist's waiting room was my father. He just sat there sipping a beer and smoking his pipe, as if everything were perfect.

Exactly one hour after we arrived, Ma stood up and said, "It's been lovely, but we must go."

Cornelia and Melissa stood up immediately. William said, "Can I hold your rifle before we go, Gran'ma?" but before Dixie could answer, Ma snapped, "No, you may not, William."

My father looked a little puzzled, but he stood up, too. I guess Ma hadn't told him that we were just going to stay one hour. Dixie looked miserable.

As I left, I gave her hand a hard squeeze. Boy! Life sure gets complicated sometimes. But I knew one thing for sure—Dixie needed to see us more than one dry hour every week or so. This kind of visit was worse than no visit at all, because everyone except my father hated it so. Okay—maybe what I meant to say was that *I* needed to see Dixie and Beagle more than one dry hour every week or so.

5

That was Sunday. Monday, we were due to meet with Mr. Kruger again for lesson number two on the trumpet. I was really looking forward to it because, to tell you the truth, I hadn't been doing too well with the trumpet on my own. I got a noise now whenever I blew into it—but it was hard for me to tell ahead of time what that noise would sound like. Each time was an adventure, and I knew *that* wasn't right.

The other nine trumpeters were already there when I arrived. Actually, they were watching the doorway as I walked in. The minute they saw me, they started talking to each other. I went up to the first clump of three.

"Hi, fellas. How'd you do this week?"

I got two stares and a mumble. "Okay."

"I think I need some help. I get a good sound, but

sometimes it's up, sometimes it's down . . . I never know. Did any of you have that trouble?"

They all shook their heads. No trouble. Three winners, right? I gave up on them. When Mr. Kruger arrived and they had to put their little lying lips up to their little trumpets, then we'd see. I moved on to a pair—short, fat, and redheaded; and tall, thin, with oily, black hair.

"Hi. How'd it go? Did you learn the music already?"

"Sure we did," Red said. "What do you think? A baby could have played *that* music."

His friend nodded. "Boy, that's nothing. Anyone who had trouble with that music is in sad shape," and they both nodded like two of those dogs people stick in the rear windows of their cars.

Okay, I thought. I don't need a brick to fall on me. No one in this room but me is going to admit that they couldn't handle their trumpets or the music. So, if I'm smart, I'll just clam up and lie low and watch—or listen, as the case might be.

Mr. Kruger came in with a kind of concentrated look on his face. He looked like my father does when the car conks out and he gets out to see if he can fix it, but he already knows he isn't going to be able to.

"Everybody is here? Good! Open your music to Exercise One, please," and we were off.

I wasn't first this time, which was fine with me. I was about third. The first two made a lot of noise, but it went in every direction—just like my noise. Mr. Kruger worked with them for a couple of minutes, showing them how to hold the trumpet and where to put it up against their mouths. I watched him like a hawk, and when my turn came, I tried to do likewise.

Well, the sounds I made were louder, but they weren't the sounds I'd hoped to make—the notes in Exercise One.

"Miss Boone, you heard what we were discussing, the first two boys and I?"

"Yes, sir."

"Good. Keep it in mind, and try to follow my suggestions. Next!"

And that was that. On to the next—period. He didn't really work with me at all.

I sat down. For the very first time, I wondered if I had done the right thing when I signed up for the trumpet. What made it worse was that I had to sit there and watch and listen while Mr. Kruger worked with everyone else. Everyone was still terrible, but if everyone got a little personal attention every week, even just a minute or two, and I never did, they were bound to pull ahead of me.

Then I got angry. Maybe I wasn't going to be a good trumpet player. Maybe they all really did find it easier than I did and I was just kidding myself that they sounded terrible, but I was as good as they were, and I was a member of this school, and I was entitled to my couple of minutes every week.

45

For the rest of the lesson, I tried to talk myself into going up to Mr. Kruger afterward and asking him to spend more time with me—but at the last minute, I couldn't. I just walked out as if it was all right that I'd been treated that way. I told myself that if it happened again, I'd say something then and there, right to his face—but inside, I wasn't absolutely sure I would. It's hard telling someone like Mr. Kruger that he's not treating you fairly. It's easier just to smile and pretend you don't mind. But I did mind.

I practiced the trumpet all week long, hard. My lips got so swollen and pink, my father winced whenever he looked at me over dinner. But I kept it up. Cornelia and Melissa complained about the noise, so I had to go to the basement to practice—which was sort of lonely and gloomy without Dixie and Stonewall Jackson and Ulysses S. Grant. Every evening after supper, my mother would say, "Time for the piano," as if she was announcing that the Baked Alaska was ready. All the rest of us would groan. I would walk into the living room, take out my music, bang the bench lid down, and start to play.

One thing about short, stubby fingers—they are *strong*. I could play loud, right from the beginning, and I did. I figured everyone would get tired of "Smiling Flowers" quicker if they couldn't get away from it. I pounded it out about twenty times every evening. Melissa and Cornelia complained about the piano, too, but Ma said they should go to the library. You don't just trot down to the cellar with a grand piano.

Band practice was exhausting. I guess Mr. Kruger expected us all to be better than we had been the week before—and we weren't. He yelled a lot, and hit the desk with his ruler, and ran his hand back over his head again and again. I think that's how he got bald. But he kept us working to the bitter end.

Mrs. Ramsbottom didn't yell, or hit anything with a ruler, or tear her hair out, but she didn't act too thrilled with my performance either. When Ma asked how it had gone, she said, "Oh, it's too early to tell yet, Mrs. Boone. We must give the child time," which I think meant, "She can only get better."

I saw Dixie and Beagle Saturday afternoon. I had to go to the store for Ma, and I ran into them in front of the drugstore. Beagle was so happy to see me, he actually barked, and Dixie said, "Billy! Honey—come on in and have a soda. My treat."

We tied Beagle up outside and got stools right near the window, where we could watch him and he could see us. I told Dixie all about Mr. Kruger and Mrs. Ramsbottom, and she said, "You aren't going to let that Mr. Kruger get away with that, are you, Billy?"

"I don't think so. I wanted to say something this time, but everyone's scared to death of him."

"Everyone but the Boones," she said. "He puts his pants on one leg at a time, child, like everyone else. Teachers are paid by people like your father, who is a very fair man. That makes Mr. Kruger just a servant of the people, which is us. We've entrusted him with a certain authority. We didn't make him God. And your father would expect him to be fair."

Well, she was right, there. My father was a fair man. All my life, since I was tiny, I'd known I could count on that. And if he and all the other parents expected Mr. Kruger to be fair, he'd just have to be fair.

I stood up. "Dixie, if he doesn't help me—just like he helps those boys—I will say something."

She nodded. "Darned right."

I walked into trumpet class feeling *very* shaky. The other nine were there, all eyes, lined up. The Owls. I didn't even bother to talk to them. Besides, I wasn't sure whether I might not throw up if I opened my mouth.

Mr. Kruger marched in and pointed to the first boy in the line. "Exercise One, please. Watch the tempo."

First boy bombed out. Mr. Kruger came down from his platform and stood beside him and worked with him till he could play a fairly clear, unwavering note. One note. But that was more than yours truly could do.

"Next!" And the bullet finger pointed to the boy beside me.

Well, he was making progress. He hit it well to

48

start with—but he wavered off into a kind of a squeak. Mr. Kruger gave him a three-minute lecture on breathing.

"Next!" Me. My heart was pounding in my throat. I wasn't sure I could even blow. My lips felt so numb! But I gave it all I had.

Have you ever stepped on a cat's tail? Well . . .

"Miss Boone, practice! You must practice if you are to succeed with *any* instrument."

Somehow, that did it. I mean, I had put in at least an hour every day—down in that basement, all by myself—and he was making it look as if I never put any effort into it at all, as if I was goofing off.

He was already pointing to the next boy. "Mr. Kruger!" I said. Actually, because I was so excited and keyed up, I think it came out louder than I meant it to.

"Yes?" The kids nearest him wilted in their seats like hot lettuce. So did I.

"I need help."

"All my students need help, Miss Boone. That is why they are here." The boys giggled, and Mr. Kruger smiled a little. I wanted to hit him, and them, so badly I bit my tongue.

"I *have* been practicing, very hard. I need you to work with me, just like you do with the rest of them—with the boys."

There was a long, long silence. Even the gigglers shut up.

"You are not satisfied with the quality of my instruction, Miss Boone?"

"I think you are the best trumpet player I ever heard, but you just kind of skip over me."

"I give you the same opportunity to play I give everybody else." His face was red now. He was getting mad.

"Yes, but then you just point your finger at someone else, and say 'Next!'"

"Miss Boone, you are dismissed from this class today. I will discuss this with you later. As a matter of fact, I would prefer to discuss this with you and one of your parents. It seems you expect preferential treatment."

I picked up my trumpet and left. Now I'd done it. At least some instruction was better than none.

The next day, my father got a call—he was the one who'd signed my permission form—asking him to come down to the school Wednesday afternoon to meet Mr. Kruger. I was supposed to be there, too.

"What's all this about, Billy?" he asked at dinner.

"Mr. Kruger thinks I want preferential treatment, Dad, but I don't. I just want him to treat me the same as the boys."

My mother said, "I knew this was a bad idea, Charles. There are just some things—"

My father said, "Why don't we wait till I've met this Mr. Kruger, Barbara? Maybe when I've heard both sides of the story, we'll know better where we're at."

My mother shook her head and started to clear. Cornelia said, "Honestly, Billy, why do you always have to stir up trouble?" William kicked her under the table. She blamed me, and I got talked to about it, but it was worth it. William is a good little kid.

I was supposed to report to Mr. Kruger's office right after school, and my father was supposed to meet us both there. My mouth was dry, and my head ached, and I hated being a kid. Here I was, wanting something so badly that I even dreamed about it all the time, and just because I was a girl, it might be taken away from me—by two other people. My father and Mr. Kruger. And I *had* tried. I really had. It was not fair. So I was nervous and mad all at the same time.

My father was in the office, with his back to me, looking out the window, when I walked in.

"Daddy?"

"Billy! What kind of day did you have, darling?"

I walked over to him, and he put his arm around my shoulders. I could feel him beside me, great big, and soft, and warm. I leaned up against him for a minute, as if I were a little kid again.

The door opened and Mr. Kruger came in.

"Good afternoon. Mr. Boone, is it? Kruger, here." He put his hand out. He was talking fast and cold, as if he knew he'd be on his way to something more important in a minute.

"Why, good afternoon, Mr. Kruger. This is a

pleasure, sir. You have certainly built an excellent reputation as a musician in our community."

"Thank you. I have always taken my work very seriously." He took a deep breath, and I thought, Here it comes.

"That's why I was so disturbed—no, offended, even—by your daughter's accusations."

My father turned to me. "What did you accuse Mr. Kruger of doing, Billy?"

"Nothing, Dad. Really. I just asked for the same time the boys got. That's all."

Mr. Kruger started to say something, but my father cut in. He speaks slow—and soft and lazy—but he gets through.

"You felt that you weren't getting exactly the same treatment as the boys?" I looked at Mr. Kruger. He seemed to be swelling up and turning red. I nodded yes.

"Billy, we are all here to get this straightened out. I'm sure Mr. Kruger is as anxious as I am to understand exactly what's wrong."

"I can tell you exactly what's wrong, Mr. Boone. Your daughter is not practicing, is not progressing. She wishes to be a star performer, yah. But she has neither the drive nor the talent to be one. This is a painful fact for her to accept, I'm sure, but . . ." and he shrugged.

Dad turned toward him slowly, like a mountain rearranging itself. "Lord, Mr. Kruger—you can tell all that from just three group lessons? You're an amazing man, sir."

"She cannot even hit and hold a single note, Mr. Boone. It's very sad, but . . ."

"I see."

"The fact is, Mr. Boone," he leaned forward toward my father, "there are very few competent female trumpeters. One might even say—none." He shrugged.

"Is that so?" My father sounded like a little kid being told that there wasn't any Santa Claus, but I knew. I could feel it. Something had happened inside him. He had just swung over to my side.

"Ach, yes. They have not the stamina, the wind, the strength. It's a well-known fact, musically. And one must attack, with the trumpet. It is like a magnificent charger, leading the way into battle. It is not a woman's instrument, you understand."

My father straightened up and cleared his throat. "I understand that Billy *has* been practicing, *has* all the drive in the world, and might make a damn fine trumpet player, given the chance. And you must understand, Mr. Kruger, that I intend to see to it that she gets that chance. I think that she is entitled to her three minutes, or five minutes, or whatever—just as much as any boy."

There was a long silence. I could hear my own heart beating.

"I cannot guarantee that your daughter will be a

good trumpet player. The school board will back me up on this, Mr. Boone."

"I'm sure they would. I'm sure all they would expect from you, or from anyone in their employ, is fair play. Now, I didn't happen to *want* Billy to play the trumpet. But she wanted it enough for both of us, and she's going to get her chance. The accident of her female birth is not going to prevent that, if I can help it. And I would match her against any boy in your trumpet section for endurance and lung power and determination. Believe me, Mr. Kruger, you are underestimating my daughter. Particularly her lung power."

Well, he didn't have to go that far, but I wasn't about to object. If my father was on my side, how could I lose?

Mr. Kruger turned and walked to the door. "I shall readmit Miss Boone to the trumpet section. She will receive exactly the same treatment as any of the others. But we will all be wasting our time, Mr. Boone . . . just wasting our time." He opened the door, marched out, and slammed the door closed behind him.

I hugged my father around the waist. "Thank you, Daddy. I didn't think you'd be on my side."

He shook his head. "Neither did I."

"I'll practice night and day. Honest. I'll be so good."

He looked unhappy. "Now, Billy, darling, don't let's overdo. An hour a day would be ample. More

54

than ample. You don't want to wear your lips out or something."

I nodded. "Okay, Daddy. An hour a day."

"And try to do it right after school, dear—before I get home."

"Sure thing, Dad."

We drove home together. No talking. I was too exhausted for words, and my father kept rubbing his forehead as if he had a headache.

6

Well, from then on, I got my three minutes in trumpet. But that was all. Like Dixie says, "You can lead a horse to water, but you cannot make him drink." We'd made Mr. Kruger give me my time, but we couldn't make him like it. He wasn't a great smiler anyway, but when he was talking to me his face was always set and hard looking, and his voice made me shiver.

In between lessons, I practiced till the neighbors complained, and Ma made me stop at forty-five minutes.

As far as the piano went, I'd had it. I didn't like the instrument, and I didn't like Mrs. Ramsbottom. She was always looking at me as if I had a rash. And I didn't like the music. It was so tinkly and la-di-da—not bright and bold and shining, like trumpet sounds. So I just pounded away for my practice time every evening, and I didn't pay too much attention to rests or tempo or even hitting the right note. They could lead *me* to the piano, but they couldn't make me love it. Ma shortened my practice time from thirty minutes to fifteen after Dad said my playing, so soon after dinner, was giving him indigestion and an ulcer.

The big blow-up came in December. I'd had my usual Saturday-morning lesson, and my mother came to pick me up. Mrs. Ramsbottom asked her to step into the kitchen and told me to stay in the living room. I sat there on her prickly sofa, wondering if she was going to spring a Christmas recital on me, and perspiring. But that wasn't it.

When Ma came out, she looked upset. She said, "Come on, Billy, and say good-bye to Mrs. Ramsbottom," and marched out.

I said, "Good-bye, Mrs. Ramsbottom. See you next week."

She just waved at me and closed the door behind me.

Once I was in the car, I said, "What did she want to talk to you about, Ma?"

"You."

"Oh? Did I do something wrong?"

"Not really. It's just that you have absolutely no talent for music at all. None. She doesn't even want to teach you any longer." She shook her head. "I never heard of someone being so bad the teacher gave up on her after only three months."

In one way, this whole thing made me nervous because I could see it had really upset Ma. Her cheeks were bright red, and she drove home with her neck and head held stiff and looking straight ahead. But in another way, I could have jumped out and run along beside the car, cheering. It was all over! No more piano. No more Mrs. Ramsbottom and her fingernail checks. No more "Smiling Flowers." What a relief! I kept a lid on it because I didn't think my mother would be too thrilled if I acted happy—but I was.

When we got home, Ma charged straight on into the house, looking for my father, I guess, to report to him. I went down to the basement where I could grin and whistle and jump up and down on the old sofa a little, to let off steam. Then I called Dixie from the kitchen phone and let her know. She wasn't as thrilled for me as I'd thought she'd be.

"Your ma must be greatly disappointed."

"She is. But she shouldn't have made me, Dixie. That's not right."

"She thought it was for your own good, hon. She wants you to grow up to be an accomplished lady."

"Well, I'm not. Not if it means playing that dumb piano, and wearing tight clothes all the time, and caring about whether or not the kitchen cabinets need new shelf paper."

Dixie said, "How's your father?"

"I haven't seen him yet this morning. He was all right last night."

"That's nice. Tell him his mother was asking after him." She stopped, and then she said, "No. Don't say that. Just tell him . . . never mind. Don't tell him anything." She sounded discouraged.

"Is everything okay, Dixie?"

"Sure, hon. See you this afternoon at the drugstore if you have to do the shopping. My treat."

"You bet!"

They called me into the living room. Big trouble. Whenever my mother and father get together and talk for a long time and then call me into the living room, that means big trouble.

"Billy, darling," my father said, "your mother has had some disturbing news. It seems Mrs. Ramsbottom has"—he made a little gesture with his hands—"washed her hands of you. She has told your mother she believes you have absolutely no musical gift—at all. Not that that matters to us, dumpling—we love you just as you are, but it does raise some questions, doesn't it?"

"What kind of questions?"

"Well, like what to do about the trumpet."

I got this sudden, clammy chill. What was he driving at?

"The fact is, Billy, that your trumpet playing places a strain on the whole neighborhood in warm weather, when the windows are open, and on this family, when they're closed. Now, if you were making progress, and we could all see that the sacrifices

59

we're making were leading somewhere, well then— it would be worth it. But if nothing's ever going to come of it, why, it's pretty hard to defend keeping it up, isn't it?"

"I'm making progress. I'm playing a lot better. You can ask Mr. Kruger."

My father winced.

My mother said, "We *know* what Mr. Kruger thinks, Billy. At the time, it sounded as if he was just against girls playing the trumpet—but now, in the light of Mrs. Ramsbottom's testimony, we're forced to conclude that any further money or time spent on music would be a total waste."

They were going to cut off my trumpet lessons! "You can't do that to me. I've worked hard, and I *am* getting better, all the time, and I love the trumpet. I'm going to be good someday. You'll see."

"Now, Billy," my father said, "no one likes to admit defeat. But the fact is that Mrs. Ramsbottom is a professional, and I've *heard* you playing the piano, dear, and you don't seem to have much of a gift for it."

"Face facts, Billy," my mother said, standing up and picking up her purse. "Music's not for you. Everybody has strengths and weaknesses. It's a part of growing up, finding out what's possible and what isn't."

I felt as if a steamroller was going over me. This wasn't right. They couldn't do this to me, so fast and easy—as if it didn't matter any more than finding out I couldn't wear a certain color. This was important to me. I yelled, "I don't want to give up the trumpet. I do too have musical ability."

My mother looked at me as if I had just fallen down and hurt myself—sad, feeling sorry for me. "Billy, darling, be realistic—"

"You don't understand. I never tried, with the piano. I didn't want to play the piano. I hated it. And I wanted to be bad so you'd let me quit."

"You mean, you let us throw away all that money. . . ." my mother said.

"And ruined my digestion," my father added.

"Deliberately?" Back to my mother again.

"I'm sorry. It's just that you were forcing me to take the piano. I hated it."

My father shook his head from side to side, like a sad, old bear. "Billy, I'm real disappointed in you. Yes, sir, I am. You don't know how I dreaded coming home every evening. . . ."

"Come now, Charles," my mother said. "It wasn't all that bad." She turned back to me. "All right, young lady. You wanted to drop the piano. You got your wish. We're also dropping the trumpet, and let this be a lesson to you. You created this situation, and now you can live with it."

"But I explained to you—"

"That's not the point anymore, Billy," my mother said. "You deceived us. Again. Deliberately. You let us waste all that money—not to mention my time every Saturday morning. And it's time you learned not to do that." She picked up the rest of her things. "As far as I am concerned, the subject is closed."

I turned back to my father. "Come on, Dad, can't I please keep on taking the trumpet? You said I could. Please?" I was almost crying, but I didn't care. He was my last hope. Ma walked out of the room.

"Billy, you should never have done this."

"You made me do it! You and Ma. All I wanted was to take the trumpet. That's all I ever wanted. She made me take the piano. And she won't let me see Dixie. Whatever I like, she won't let me do. I hate her. And I wish I were dead." I ran out of the living room and into the bathroom and locked the door. I guess I stayed in there an hour, crying, with the water running into the sink so no one could hear me. I wouldn't give her the satisfaction.

7

Well, sooner or later, everyone has to come out of
the bathroom, right? But if they were going to
blight my life, and take away my trumpet, no law
said I had to act like I was enjoying it. Whenever I
felt sad or angry, I just let it show. I didn't put on a
sunny little smile. I just looked like I felt. When I
didn't want to eat, I didn't—and even when I did
want to, I didn't. A small part of me, which sounded
a lot like my mother, kept saying that I was being
very childish. But the rest of me drowned that part
out. If they were going to treat me as if I had no
right to a vote, even over things that really affected
me, if they were going to force me to do things and
then punish me for not doing them well, then I was
all through pretending or cooperating. And if they
got worried about my not eating—let them. They

should know how it felt to be me right now. A little worry would be nothing!

Monday, at breakfast, Ma said, "Bologna or ham on your sandwich, Billy?" and I sighed and said, "Don't trouble yourself, Ma. I'm not hungry."

"Not now, maybe," she said, "but by lunchtime." She was smiling her gracious smile. Big deal. She was just letting me know she was not going to be disturbed by my not eating.

"I'm not hungry now. I will not be hungry later. You'll just be wasting a sandwich."

My father slammed his fist down onto the table so hard all the coffee cups jumped into the air. "Damn! I've had about all I can take of this." I said earlier that he didn't usually yell, and he didn't. But this morning he did.

"Charles, Billy's just trying to manipulate you," my mother said.

"Of course she is. I know that! The point is, it's working."

"You're not going to give in. . . ."

"Now see here, Barbara—maybe we underestimated Billy's need to play that thing. Maybe, without in any way excusing what she did," he turned toward me and gave me a dark look, "without in any way condoning the lowdown . . . sneaky . . . underhanded . . . way she fought us on the piano," he eased his hand over his stomach as if it still hurt him, "we can work out a compromise here."

"I will not stand for giving in to her, Charles."

"And I will not stand for living in the middle of a battlefield. A man's got to have some peace in his own house."

Now they were both yelling. I felt terrible. I was responsible. I'd never wanted it to come to this. I hated it when they argued—particularly over me.

"Could I say something?"

"No!" They both yelled at me. I got up and ran out of the kitchen. Cornelia and Melissa were standing in the hall, listening.

"Now, you've done it, Billy," Melissa said.

"You ought to be ashamed of yourself," Cornelia said. "See what you've started."

I took off down the hall and out the front door. I could still hear them going at it. I ran straight down the road, and didn't stop till I got to Dixie's house. She opened the door on the second knock, and I grabbed her and hung on, crying and talking all at once—just a big, blubbering mess.

The phone rang about half an hour later, about the time I'd gotten my nose blown clear and my face washed. It was my father. I could tell right away, from Dixie's voice.

"Yes. Yes. She's here and everything's all right."

He talked a long time. I could hear a low rumble, even sitting across the table.

"I'll tell her. And Beagle and I will see that she eats and gets to school later in the morning."

I grabbed Dixie's arm. "Tell him I'm sorry. Tell him that I love him."

65

Dixie said, "Charles, Billy's terribly sorry about all this. She says she loves you."

There was a short, soft rumble. Dixie hung up.

"He loves you, too, hon. Let's have a little light breakfast."

"What did he say, Dixie? Earlier."

"He said he had a plan you might agree to. He and your mother had worked it out. I gathered everything up at the big house is calm as a millpond now. He wants to talk to you about it after school—down at his office. Cereal?"

"Yes, please. Did he say if the plan meant I could play the trumpet again?"

"No. He did not. But he did say to go on to trumpet class, as usual. He'll drop your trumpet off at the school, and you can pick it up at the office. That sounds promising. Eggs?"

"One, please. Have you got a quarter you can give me for milk? Oh, and a quarter for the bus, downtown, after school?"

"Sure thing. Toast with the eggs?"

"Yes, please. Is there any juice?"

"In the icebox. Help yourself. How about a little frizzled ham?"

"Sure. I love the way you do the ham. Dixie—I didn't mean to make them fight like that."

"They know that, Billy. You were just backed into a corner, and you used everything you had to fight back with. It wasn't something you set up

66

yourself. It was a three-way thing. Your dad, and your mother, and you."

"It scares me when they fight."

She nodded. "Sure it does. You're afraid things might change. They might separate, or get a divorce even—and then what would happen to you?" She set my plate down in front of me and stepped back. "It's just about impossible for any two or three people to be locked in, real close together, and not fight sometimes. God made us all different, and nature made every one of us mainly interested in keeping our own selves going. So—there's going to be a little shouting and cussing every now and then."

"Do *you* think they'll ever get a divorce, Dixie?"

"No, I don't. And I'll tell you why. Because I've seen them come through some rough times, even way before you were born, and when things got bad—really bad—why, they pulled together like a pair of matched mules. All this spitting and spatting is just on the surface. Underneath, they need each other, and they respect each other. Doesn't sound like much, but it's just about everything. And the longer they live with each other, the more they like each other. They're different as they can be, but that's the way they wanted it."

I finished my breakfast, and then we walked to school—the three of us, going slow for Beagle, who had to check out every tree, every bush, and every tall blade of grass. What a dog!

67

When it came time for my trumpet class, I walked down the corridor thinking, I wonder if I'll be doing this next week. It made me kind of trembly. Then I thought, Whatever Dad's plan is, I'll do it if I possibly can.

Mr. Kruger called on me first. I picked up my shining trumpet. This might be the very last time I got to do this. I put it up to my lips, and I let her rip on Exercise Nine.

Even Mr. Kruger was surprised. I could see that. His eyebrows went up.

He came over to my chair and said, "I see you have finally decided to buckle down and practice, Miss Boone. Good! Keep up with the practicing. You'll never get anywhere without it. Next." Which, from him, was practically a pat on the back. I sat down, feeling terribly happy—to have impressed Mr. Kruger!—and terribly sad, in case I was never going to get another chance to impress him.

My father's office is in a little old building called The Arcade. The Arcade is about a hundred and fifty years old. It's made of wood and brick and marble columns. People pass through it, on the ground floor, to get from one street to the next. It's sort of like a gigantic breezeway lined with shops and offices. It has a colored-glass roof, and a strip of ground down the middle with plants and a fountain, and old-fashioned street lights. My father's office is on the second floor, up one flight of rickety old steps.

I went right on in because the receptionist, Miss Claridge, knows me and usually just waves at me to keep on going.

My father looked up from his papers. "Billy. Are you feeling any better?"

"Yes. I am. And Mr. Kruger said I was doing better in trumpet today. Really, he did, Dad."

"That's good, Billy." He ran the tips of his fingers back and forth along his pen. "Billy, honey, I've got a proposition for you. You're free to take it or leave it. It makes no difference to me, one way or the other."

"Yes, Dad?"

"Well, as you know—maybe you don't—anyhow, James Bowden, the janitor who normally cleans my offices and several others on this floor, has come to work lately with liquor on his breath. As a matter of fact, he was slightly inebriated." He put up his hand. "Now, I have a drink every evening myself, as you know, and on weekends your mother and I . . . well, that's neither here nor there, but I felt that James should not be working in this building drunk and smoking cigarettes. The Arcade could go up like kindling. I spoke to James about it once, and he was surly—very surly. So, since he refused to cooperate, I have been forced to let him go."

"Wow!"

"It is my forlorn hope that the fear of being let go

by others in this building will convince him to restrict his drinking to the hours *after* work."

"Did you tell the others?"

"Not yet. I'd like to give James a chance to change his mind first. The point is, I am now without any janitorial service at all. The other janitor who works The Arcade, Mr. Hennessey, has all the work he can handle. So it occurred to me that you might want to assume James's duties. The money you earn can go toward your trumpet lessons and the trumpet rental and, eventually, your own trumpet. *If* the arrangement proves satisfactory to all parties."

"What if James Bowden wants his job back? I want to take the trumpet, but I don't want to take a job away from someone who really needs it."

"Don't worry about it, Billy. It's my understanding that James has quite a few small contracts all over town. He can probably pick up another one any time he wishes to. As long as I'm happy with your work, you have the job."

I sat there thinking it over for maybe ten seconds. Then I said, "I'll take it."

"I thought you would."

"When do I start?"

"Today. I'll show you what I want you to do. Your mother can give you ideas on the best products to use and all that."

"How many days a week, Dad?"

"Let's say Mondays and Wednesdays, after school. An hour each day should do it."

70

"That's wonderful! Oh, boy. And this is okay with Ma?"

"I give you my word. She was all in favor of it. She feels that you will benefit from closer contact with domestic duties."

"Oh, boy."

"That'll do, Billy. She's absolutely right. You're twelve years old, now—plenty old enough to be learning some of the womanly skills."

I wanted to say more, but I didn't dare. Nothing else mattered as much as taking the trumpet. If I picked up a womanly skill here and there, so what? I could always drop it again later.

"One thing, Billy. There is a lot of responsibility connected even with this small job. I have some important papers here and some very expensive business machinery. You're going to have to be careful not to throw out something vital. The old janitor— the one I had till six months ago, when he retired and James took the job—watched every scrap of paper go by him as he emptied the baskets into the chute. Twice he caught and saved documents that had somehow slipped off people's desks. When you're cleaning the copier and the typewriters and such, you're going to have to be really careful. If you knock an electric typewriter onto the floor, I'll have a bill for repairs that will eat up your pay for six months."

"I understand."

He sighed and stood up. "Then why do I have this feeling that I'm boarding the *Titanic*?"

71

I knew he was only kidding.

"Come on, Billy. We can start in the file and supply closet. . . ."

Who would ever have guessed it would take so many different sizes and kinds of paper and envelopes just to run one small law office? When my father opened the closet door, I thought we must be looking at last week's trash. It looked like a tornado had hit a stationery store.

"First, you'd better sort all this out."

I didn't actually say, "You're kidding!" but I was thinking it. There goes an hour, easy, just on paperwork.

"See the little labels on the edges of the shelves, Billy? Well, each label describes what should go above it. If you can read the labels, you can sort it all out. Easy as falling off a log. . . ."

Off a log, into a bog! I think I groaned out load. Well, a person's got to be able to express herself.

"How'd it get like this?" I asked, real casual.

He waved a hand in the air. "Oh, you know. Miss Claridge and I are awfully busy sometimes—and that little girl who came in to help Miss Claridge every afternoon has moved. And Mrs. Ottoman has been out sick for a week." He cleared his throat. "James didn't actually work *inside* the cabinets, but I thought, since you'd be here, anyway. . . ."

I could see the handwriting on this wall, all right. Whenever Mrs. Ottoman was out sick, yours truly would get the supply closet in the neck. I prayed that Mrs. Ottoman would get well fast and stay healthy.

"Now, over here, where Mrs. Ottoman usually sits, you can start sweeping and dusting and all that." And he waved his hand again, this time at the windows.

"I clean the windows, too?" Not that they didn't need it. They were so dirty, they looked like frosted glass.

"James did." He sounded hurt.

"*When* did he?"

"Now, Billy, if I'm going to have to argue with you over every little thing. . . ."

"Sorry, Dad. I'll do the windows." I had to keep remembering that trumpet.

"And when you get to the trash baskets, Billy, be awfully careful to get up all the crumbs, and make sure there's no food left in the bottoms of the baskets." He bent down. "We've had a little problem lately."

"What kind of problem, Dad?"

"Well, mostly mice. This is an old building, and being in the city and all . . ."

Okay. I could handle that. I don't mind mice too much if *I* see them first. It's when they startle me that I get a little tense.

He leaned down a little lower. "And roaches. Just every so often, mind you, but we don't want them to get a foothold, do we?"

No, we didn't. I really do mind roaches . . . a lot.

I don't like things that crunch when you step on them.

We moved on. "Be sure to dust all the machines thoroughly—and straighten up the magazines in the reception area."

"Right."

"And then there's the bathroom. I believe James went over it once lightly on Mondays and gave it a real good cleaning on Wednesdays."

I hadn't counted on the bathroom. The trumpet wavered in front of my eyes—and I wondered if it was worth it. I don't even like cleaning the john at home.

I opened the bathroom door. Yup. All the usual things, except a tub.

"Do I have to?"

"You do, if you want the job."

I thought it over. Twenty seconds, maybe. "Okay, Dad. You've got a deal." And we shook on it. "How much?"

"Well, let's see how you do, first, Billy—and how long it takes. I can't pay too much."

"Will I make as much as James?"

"No. You will not. I did not have to feed James, or buy him a new T-shirt every week, or take him to the movies. If you make enough to pay for your trumpet lessons and rental, with maybe a little bit left over, you'll be doing well."

Boy, Dad gets so heated over little things sometimes.

I spent the next hour on the supply cabinet. Even while I was still working on it, Dad and Miss Claridge kept coming over and taking stuff, and when they pulled out the wrong thing, they weren't any too careful where they put it back. I could see how the closet had gotten to be such a mess. I said something once or twice, like "Hey! That doesn't go there," or "*Third* shelf—not the top shelf," but what would they do when I wasn't there? Slip right back into their old ways. So, just before I left for the day, I made up a couple of signs and taped them to the closet door, inside and out, and to the shelves. "DON'T LITTER!" "NEATNESS COUNTS," and "I'LL BE BACK WEDNESDAY," which I hung from the middle shelf, as a warning—sort of like the mark of Zorro. I did that one in red.

After I'd tidied the supply cabinet, I started sweeping. When I got to the trash baskets, I understood why they had had "little problems." When I emptied them, I found a two-inch crust in the bottom of each one, made of cigar and pipe ashes, Danish pastry crumbs, and fruit pits. There was also a sprinkling of these items between each basket and the wall behind it. Talk about Mouse Heaven! I took the baskets downstairs to the restaurant and put some hot water and soap in each one and left them there to soak a while, until I finished sweeping.

When I came back to empty them, I was stumped. I couldn't pour that stuff down a john—it would clog up the plumbing for the whole building. So I took them out to the curb, one at a time, when the cop at the corner wasn't looking, and emptied them into the gutter between two parked cars, and got back into the building in a hurry. By the time the red tide had reached his corner, I was all through and the baskets and I were upstairs, drying off.

I put fresh newspapers in the bottom of each one and went in and told my father that he and Miss Claridge would have to knock it off or I would not be responsible. No more eating in the office!

He said, "Billy, we have to have our coffee breaks."

I gave him a look. "Coffee" was not the problem.

He drove me home, of course. I was so tired, I didn't even talk.

When we walked in, Ma said, "Well, how did it go at the office?"

Dad said, "A new broom sure as hell sweeps clean," and went to get his beer.

I said, "I have to do the bathroom, even."

"Of course, Billy. It has to be done regularly. That's very important."

I made a face.

She said, "Well, if we want some things in life, we have to be willing to work for them."

I gave up. I wasn't going to get any sympathy from someone who washes the plastic playing cards with the dessert dishes after each bridge game. She was just enjoying this. I went in and lay down to wait for supper.

After dinner, I called Dixie from the hall while everyone was watching TV. I told her about the new job. She made sympathetic clucking noises. When I finished, she said, "I love Charles. He's one man in a thousand, Billy. But he's not perfect. He could pay a little more attention to his mother, for one thing. And he always was untidy."

I nodded—not that she could see a nod over the phone.

"When he was a boy, I just dreaded going through his pockets. I think I got warts once, from a frog he'd carried around for a week before I found it. I dug out more stuff! He had one pocket that he couldn't use, it was so glued shut with gum."

I laughed, but she said, "I'm not kidding, Billy. I could not get that pocket open, so for months he wore it stiff and sealed shut. Chafed him something terrible on hot days . . . but he never learned."

He never learned. I could just see what that supply closet would be like by Wednesday. I said goodnight and hung up.

Tuesday afternoon, after school, Ma took me shopping for my job. The idea was to outfit me as a janitress.

We started with an apron, which was supposed to make me look real professional and keep my school clothes clean. I found a lovely striped one—red, blue, yellow, and white, with big brass buttons—but she said that it would be too hard on my father's eyes. *She* picked out one made of blue and white mattress ticking. I held out quite a while, since I was the one who had to wear it, and I did *not* want to appear in public looking like a camp cot, but she won, in the end, because she had the charge card.

We moved on to the household products. All those years when I had tuned out the TV commercials, maybe I should have been listening. Naturally, she picked out her favorites—floor wax, floor cleaner, wall cleaner, dusting spray, sponges, paper towels, window cleaner, scouring powder . . . the large, economy size in everything. I could hardly lift it all. When I realized that my own hands were going to have to scrub, rub, or spread every ounce of every product onto something in Dad's office, I was depressed. It was as if an endless road of dirty surfaces stretched out in front of me.

That was Tuesday. Wednesday morning, my father took all that stuff to his office in the car. I thought he was going to have to make two trips.

I got to the office in the middle of the afternoon. Everything was there waiting for me, including, I noticed, a fresh layer of crumbs and pits around the baskets, and the paper snowstorm in the supply closet. Personally, I could understand why James took to drinking. Nothing in his line of work ever stayed done.

I started with the supplies. After I got everything back in place, I tried to think of some way to keep it there. If I could just sort of slow Miss Claridge and

Dad down a little, make them take a minute and pay attention, they might pick up the right thing from the start—or at least remember to put it back, if they didn't.

Then I had my brightest idea. I couldn't get it all together this afternoon—but I could come back Thursday and finish up then.

In the meantime, there was the sweeping and the dusting. When all the crumbs were swept up, I emptied the baskets down the chute and cleaned one window. One a day was plenty, even with Ma's favorite glass cleaner. I came to the conclusion, as I tried to rub the aching out of my arm, that those women in the commercials with the big smiles and the cheerful little songs about how they just loved doing windows now that Glassy Shine had come into their lives were lying through their false teeth.

Thursday afternoon I went right home from school and found about twenty nice, flat-bottomed rocks in the backyard. I scrubbed them and dried them with paper towels. Carrying them, and getting up onto the bus with them, was going to be a real problem, so I bribed William to help me—it cost me a quarter, plus his bus fare, but it was worth it. We got to Dad's office just as he and Miss Claridge were finishing up for the day.

"Billy! And William, too. This is a pleasant surprise. You looking for a ride home?"

"Sure, Dad. But I have to finish up the supply closet first."

"Oh. All right. I've got a few phone calls to make. There are some new magazines in the reception area, William."

I put a nice, clean rock on top of the paper or envelopes in each stationery box—and then I tested the system. When I reached for a piece of paper, I had to slow down and lift the rock and then put it down again—and it *did* make me think—no doubt about it. I was satisfied. I figured I'd just saved myself about two hours of work every week.

We were all standing on the balcony outside Dad's office, waiting for him to lock up, when he remembered he'd forgotten his briefcase.

"Just a minute," he said, and charged back into the office.

William leaned over the railing and said, "I'll bet I can throw a penny into the fountain from here."

Miss Claridge said, "Don't do that, William. You might hit someone."

William said, "Not if I lean over far enough."

Knowing William as I do, I made a grab for him, and it's just a blessing that I did, because it was right at that moment that my father yelled.

It was the kind of yell that makes you jump. People all over The Arcade jumped. William jumped—which is why it's a good thing I had a grip on him. I jumped. Then we all tore back into the office.

My father was over in the corner, hopping around

on one foot, holding the other between his hands. I shoved a chair up behind him and into the back of his knee, so he'd sit down on it before he fell and hurt himself.

Miss Claridge said, "What on earth?"

"Something fell on my foot! I think it's broken. I was just reaching for some paper, and something fell on my foot."

Suddenly, I had that feeling you get in your stomach when the elevator goes from the first floor to the twenty-fifth floor in ten seconds or less.

William said, "It was a rock, Dad," and held it up. One of my best rocks. From the top shelf.

"Don't be silly, William." My father turned toward the supply closet. "What would a rock be doing . . . ?"

"It's one of Billy's. To hold your papers down."

"I can explain, Dad. See—I thought that if you and Miss Claridge had to stop and lift a rock every time, you'd be more careful, and the supplies wouldn't get in such a mess."

"You put *rocks* in my supply closet?"

William said, "Sure, Dad. The whole closet's full of them."

Miss Claridge said, "Oh, Billy."

"Well, I was just trying to help. If you and Dad hadn't made such a mess of it all the time . . ."

My father said, "Miss Claridge, would you please call Dr. Toohey, and then drive me over to his office and take the kids home?"

She nodded and went to the phone.

I said, "Is there anything I can do, Dad?"

He just shook his head. Then he went back to hugging his foot. Nobody said much during the drive to Dr. Toohey's.

Miss Claridge helped Dad into the office. He made us stay in the car. Miss Claridge called our house from the office, to let Ma know we were on our way, and once Dad was being x-rayed and taken care of and all, she came out and drove us the rest of the way home.

8

As I walked in the front door, Cornelia passed me and said, "Honestly, Billy, you are the limit!"

Well, that was no big thing, because Cornelia is always saying that to me.

I walked into the kitchen and Melissa, who was making herself a cup of coffee, said, "Billy, you have just got to stop acting so crazy," which I thought was very unfair because after all, people have been using paperweights for hundreds of years—maybe thousands—and the only difference was that mine were free and came out of the back-yard, and were a surprise.

My mother came into the kitchen and said, "Melissa, I wish to speak to Billy. Privately."

I said, "Hello, Ma."

"Sit down, Billy." She sounded mad. "Billy, you did want that job at your father's office, didn't you?"

"Sure I did."

"Then why would you do a thing like that?—booby-trapping your father's supply closet."

"I didn't booby-trap it, Ma. I was just trying to keep the supplies neat."

She shook her head. "Maybe you'd better start at the beginning. Miss Claridge said rocks *you* put there were falling out of the closet onto your father. I had trouble understanding her."

I sighed. Better go all the way back to the beginning.

"Every time I went down there, the papers were all every which way. Dad and Miss Claridge were just pulling them out and throwing them back, and I thought if they had to slow down, and lift a paperweight rock each time, and then put it back, they'd be more careful."

"Is this the truth, Billy?"

"Yes. I just forgot to tell Dad. I was only trying to help. Honest, Ma. That closet was an awful mess."

And then Ma did a strange thing. She started to laugh. She laughed till she cried. I couldn't believe it. When she got her breath back, she said, "All these years, Billy, he's left the linen closet a mess, and his bureau drawers a mess, and the magazines and books in his study a mess, and the big desk in the living room a mess." She laughed some more. "I should have sent out for some rocks right at the start," and she was off again.

Parents are very odd. I will never understand

them. Here's this woman, who's supposed to admire and need and love my father so much, who's just been so mad at me for maybe breaking my father's foot—and she is hysterical and rolling on the floor, practically, because all I was trying to do was make my father keep his supplies neat. I love my mother very much—but she is a strange woman.

After a minute or two, I started to laugh, too. I couldn't help it. When someone else laughs, I could be dying, but I've got to join in.

Naturally, when Dr. Toohey brought my father home, with one foot all done up in a cast, we weren't laughing. Ma was in the kitchen stirring something that scorched very easily, so I met him at the door.

"I'm sorry, Dad. I would never hurt you on purpose."

"I know that, Billy."

"Do I still have the job?"

"Oh, Billy . . ."

"Please, Dad. I *need* the money for the trumpet."

"Why don't I just give you the money, hon, and we'll see what you can do around the house, here, to help your ma."

My mother's voice came out of the kitchen like a police siren. "Oh, no you don't! I think we should all stick to the original agreement, Charles. It will be good for Billy's character."

My father groaned. "Oh, yes. It'll be good for Billy's character, and it'll be like manna from heaven for Dr. Toohey. I don't know if I can expect Miss Claridge to stay on." He started to hobble down the hall. His voice trailed behind him. "When she opened the supply closet Tuesday morning, and that red-lettered sign fluttered out at her, I thought she was going to pass out. And now this . . ." The bathroom door closed behind him, but I could still hear a sad little rumble coming from that direction.

My mother came out of the kitchen and went to the bathroom door. "I've fixed all your favorite things, Charles. Can you eat?"

"Yes, Barbara. I can eat. I got hit on the foot, not in the mouth." There was a short pause. "Thank God."

So, I knew he was going to be all right, and I still had my job—and my trumpet. But I'd have to figure out some other way to keep the supply closet from getting messy.

9

By Monday, my father's foot didn't throb at all, unless he kept it down near the floor for more than five or ten minutes. Cornelia and Melissa had gotten so they could pass me without making some remark, like "How's Daddy's little helper this morning?" William was still pestering me to come up with a brand new idea for the closet, but my mother had said no more ideas for a while . . . at least until my father's foot healed. Then she giggled. My father was making a big effort to be nice about it. He did try, twice, to talk me out of working at the office, but I knew that he needed me. In a week, that place would be overrun with mice and roaches and knee-deep in paper. I went to school with my trumpet, feeling good.

This time, when Mr. Kruger called on me, I was confident. I knew I could do it. I really gave it all I had—three exercises, straight through, without stopping.

"Very much improved, Miss Boone. I see you are continuing to practice."

"Yes, sir, Mr. Kruger."

"If you will hold the trumpet a little higher—like so—I think you will find it easier."

I did the exercises again, holding the trumpet a little higher.

"Good. Excellent. I must say, Miss Boone, you have an astonishing lung capacity . . . for a girl."

"Thank you, Mr. Kruger."

"Next."

I was on my way. I was going to be a good trumpet player. I could feel it in my bones, and also in my lips and nasal passages.

When the class was over, one of the boys said to another, "That's not the kind of girl I like." He said it in that tone you use when you want your voice to really carry. I knew who he meant.

His buddy said, "Boy, I'll bet she lifts weights and everything."

I could feel myself blushing, and I hated that. I did not want them to know that anything they said bothered me. I kept my head down and stacked my books.

"She's so pushy. Nobody likes a pushy girl. My brother, Archie, says he won't even date a pushy girl."

Boy! who would even *want* to date his brother Archie, who has a ring around his collar, and also around his neck. But still, I was glad to get out of room 116 that afternoon.

Dixie and I got together almost every Saturday afternoon, after I'd done the grocery shopping from a list my mother gave me. We'd sit near the drugstore window and have a milk shake each, while Beagle drooled on the pavement outside. Then we'd go back out and give him a small ice-cream cone. Fair is fair.

Anyhow, we were sitting there, inhaling our shakes, and talking about men and boys and life, when my mother walked up the sidewalk, right past our window.

I ducked. What a dumb thing to do! But I didn't want her to see me sitting there with Dixie, in case she put two and two together, and figured out we were getting together every Saturday, and wanted us to stop. When I'm feeling guilty, I panic so easily. And, naturally, she had just realized that the dog tied to the bus bench was Beagle, and was peering in the window when I started to duck. Oh, boy!

For just a second, we sort of froze there—Ma outside, looking in to see if Dixie was in the drugstore, and me, inside, looking out, ducking down. She saw me. Our eyes met, just for a moment. Then she turned away and walked on past the drugstore, much faster.

"My mother just went by, Dixie. She saw me."

"Well, why didn't you wave to her to come in?"

"I was scrunching down."

"Oh." There was a long, sickening silence. "Did she see that, do you think?"

"Yes."

Another silence. I pushed my shake away. Who could eat at a time like this?

"And then she went on?"

"Yes. Only faster."

"Lord, Lord."

"What'll I do, Dixie?"

"I think you'd better go on home, hon, and talk to your ma."

"The reason I scrunched down is, I didn't want her to know that I was coming in here every Saturday . . . she might think I was goofing off."

"Would it do any good if I came along—to talk to her?"

"No!"

"Billy, doesn't your ma want you to see me at all?"

"No, really, she doesn't feel that way at all. It's just that there's a lot to do at home on Saturdays. It's the day when we get caught up and do the cleaning . . . and the shopping . . ."

"Okay. Don't take on so. I understand."

"Well, I guess I'll just go on home now."

"You do that. Just tell your ma I said I'd treat you to a shake. She'll understand."

"See you, Dixie."

She gave me a quick, dry little kiss on the cheek. "And pass *that* along to your father."

Ma was in the kitchen, peeling things for supper, when I walked in. Her cheeks were red, so I knew she was either very angry or very sad, and ready to cry.

"Hi, Ma. Was that you passing the drugstore?"

"It was. Was that you trying to hide?"

"Aw, Ma . . ."

She put the potato and the peeler down and turned around to face me. "I've had a lot of bad moments raising my children, but I've never had one of them try to hide when they saw me coming. I was never so humiliated in my life."

Well, not to make a big thing out of it, but the only reason she hadn't seen any of her other children trying to hide was that they were better at it than I was. I'd like a nickel for every time I've seen Cornelia and Melissa or William scoot when they heard Ma coming and they knew she had work on her mind.

"I'm sorry, Ma. I guess I just felt guilty that I was taking it easy. You know."

"With your grandmother."

"Yes. With Dixie. What was wrong with that? She said to come on in, she'd buy me a shake—and I was tired—so we just sat down."

"If there was nothing wrong, why did you duck when you saw me? You were certainly feeling very

91

guilty about something—something more important than sitting down to rest."

"I wasn't feeling all *that* guilty. I just ducked. I said I was sorry."

"Don't you sass me, young lady."

"Well, it's not fair. I'd done your shopping. I'd done everything you told me to do. What's wrong with having a milk shake with my own grand-mother?"

"In the first place, it's not *my* shopping. Those groceries are to feed everybody, including you. And in the second place, when people act guilty, there is a reason."

"Not always. Sometimes other people just make them *feel* guilty—for no reason."

"And what is that supposed to mean?"

"I don't know." I started to cry. I hate to cry in front of anyone. It embarrasses me.

"I'll tell you how it looked to me, Billy. It looked to me like a conspiracy—with you and your grand-mother making a fool out of me . . . sneaking around behind my back, then trying to hide when I came by."

"Dixie is not trying to make a fool out of you. She's a wonderful person. You just don't like her. She never says a bad thing about you—never!"

"She doesn't have to. All she has to do is be there—with all the time in the world to listen to you, and no real responsibility for you, so she can always just smile and say, 'Yes, sweetie, sure thing.'

I'm wearing myself out trying to do ten different things at once while she's giving you milk shakes and those awful, sickening cookies. What does she care if your teeth rot out, or if your appetite is ruined, or if you grow up not fit to do anything useful? She can always indulge you. No wonder you think she's so wonderful. If I had nothing to do all day but sit and watch TV and eat and drink . . . you'd think I was wonderful, too."

By now, we were both red in the face and crying. I wanted to reach out and touch my mother and say something right, for a change, because suddenly I could see how upset and tired she was and why she felt the way she did about Dixie—even if she was wrong. But just as I started toward her, she ran out of the kitchen. I heard her bedroom door slam hard behind her.

My father opened the kitchen door and poked his head in. "Is everything all right in here, Billy?"

I sniffled and said, "Gran'ma told me to give you this," and I walked over and kissed him, and hurried on past him to my room, bawling like a first grader on the first day of school.

I could hear him walking down the hall muttering, "Lord, Lord."

Amen.

10

Things were cool around the house for a while after that. Ma was speaking to me, but only just.

The trumpet lessons were going well. Mr. Kruger hinted that some of us might even be permitted to come and listen to the marching band practice on Thursday afternoons. When he got to me that day, he said, "I assume you have kept your Thursday afternoons free, Miss Boone."

"Yes, sir!"

After that lesson there were some more remarks about pushy girls who didn't even know how to act. Well, this pushy girl was going to get into Mr. Kruger's band some day, so let them talk. It would have been nicer if I'd had some friends in the group. But Dixie always said, "Sometimes being right is a lonely occupation," and she was right. One boy, very quiet, with sandy hair clipped short, would

94

smile at me now and then. And I noticed that he never joined in on the "Give Billy Boone the Needle" chorus. His name was George Chaffee. I found his picture in last year's yearbook, and cut it out, and pasted it onto the base of the table lamp beside my bed. George has a nice face.

The job at Dad's office was going along very well. There *was* a while there when Dad would sort of wince when he saw me coming in, but he was getting over that.

It certainly took more than one hour a day, twice a week, though. I came in at three-thirty Mondays and worked till Dad drove me home at five. That's an hour and a half, right there. On Wednesdays I got there at three-thirty and worked straight through till almost five-thirty, which is almost two hours. Of course my first job, every afternoon, was to go down to Mr. Taglione's restaurant on the first floor and get coffee and Danish for everyone. I tried to stamp all that out, but I met a lot of resistance. So I figured if you can't beat them, you might as well join them. That wasn't really work, either, because Mr. Taglione was so nice to me.

He'd yell, "Hey, Billy!" That's how he talked to me, even if we'd just finished talking about something else and I was standing three feet away. "Hey, Billy!"

Starting in March, my father went over to Mrs. Steere's house every Wednesday afternoon at four.

Mrs. Steere is very old, and very rich, and she asked my father to handle her affairs because he came from the South and so did she, and they liked each other. My father told her that there were other lawyers who had a lot more estate experience then he had had, but she didn't care. So, at four he would leave for Mrs. Steere's. Mrs. Ottoman and Miss Claridge and I would keep on working till five. They would leave at five, and I was supposed to stay in the office, working, till five-twenty, when I was supposed to lock up and go on down to the corner. My father would drive by the corner right after five-thirty and pick me up.

Some Wednesdays Mr. Taglione would say, "Hey, Billy! When you're all through up there, you lock up and come down and wait for your daddy here. I got some leftover Danish I'll let you have—half price. I got fresh ones coming in the morning." And everybody at the counter would smile, but I didn't mind, because he was so nice, and his Danish, even slightly stale, were delicious . . . and by the time I did come down, all the smilers would have gone on home.

Anyhow, it worked out so that, counting the time I spent going down to Mr. Taglione's, I was putting in almost three and a half hours, not two, but playing the trumpet was worth it. And I was getting to know more about Dad's business and seeing him as someone who was a real good lawyer who was respected and consulted by some very important people.

Dad had picked me up one Wednesday afternoon, as usual, and we'd gone home together to dinner. Actually, I'd had two Danish at Mr. Taglione's at five-fifteen, so I wasn't very hungry. We were sitting down at the table when the phone rang. As usual, Cornelia and Melissa fell all over each other trying to get to it first.

It was the police, for Dad.

We heard him say, "Yes. Yes. You don't say. Well, I'll be right down. Yes, I'd appreciate that, sir. Thank you," which told us nothing. We were all sitting on the edges of our chairs by the time he hung up.

"The office was broken into."

Everybody said, "Ooh," or "Aah," or "For heaven's sake!" William said, "Hey, that's neat. Can I go down with you?"

"Two juveniles were spotted carrying my electric typewriters away. The policeman on the corner approached them to ask them a few questions, and they started to run. He gave chase—and they were apprehended."

We all went through our "Ooh" and "Aah" routine again, because it really was kind of exciting. I was hoping he'd let me go, too, when he and William went to the office.

"They did a good deal of damage, first—looking for money, apparently."

Ma said, "Did you leave much down there, Charles?"

"No. Just a little petty cash."

Something was wrong, here. He was holding something back. His voice was strange. What else could have happened, for Pete's sake?

"They said the idea of looting the office occurred to them when they passed my door, about five-thirty, and noticed that it was ajar. The lights were all out, but the door had not been properly closed and locked."

Ma said, "Oh, Charles."

Cornelia and Melissa looked at me as if I had run over someone's pet puppy.

"That's not true, Dad. I did lock it. I lock up every Wednesday. I am *so* careful."

"Well, we'll see. I'll go down now, and you'd better come with me, Billy. William, you stay here. The rest of you may as well enjoy your dinner."

"I'll save you something, Charles," my mother said.

I got up and followed him out of the dining room, trying to catch up with him. "Daddy, you do believe me, don't you? I did lock up."

"Let's just go to the office, Billy, and see what the story is."

I went out and sat in the car. He would not say he believed me. And I had locked up. I'd finished my

98

window for the day, and I'd turned off the lights. I remembered doing that. And then I had locked the door and run down the steps to Mr. Taglione's restaurant for my Danish. I could almost see the key turning in the lock. Or was that *last* Wednesday? Had I locked up? Maybe I'd been in such a rush to get to the Danish I had forgotten. I remembered thinking that it would take some time to eat *two* of those big Danish pastries. Mr. Taglione had said there would be a couple of them. Had I been in such a hurry I'd just turned off the lights and gone? Most of the time, during the business day, the outer office door was left wide open, or, if The Arcade was really noisy, at least ajar, so people would feel comfortable about coming in for the first time. Some people feel the same way about going to a lawyer that they do about going to the dentist. Dad got a lot of what he called "drop-in" trade that way. Did I just tear out of there and leave the door half open? I could feel myself sweating—a cold, chilly sweat.

The policeman on the corner, who'd chased the suspects and caught up with them, was waiting for us in the reception area.

When I saw the inner offices I just gulped. Papers and desk supplies were thrown everywhere, like a thick, white carpet. My father's petty-cash box was on the floor, too. It had been pried open with something, and lay there gaping at me, like an empty mouth. The copier was on the floor, on its side. It was so dented, it had five sides, now, instead of four. My father's beautiful books, with their gorgeous dark red and deep blue leather bindings, were just dumped on the floor behind his desk. A couple of them were so splayed out, you knew their backs were broken. Mrs. Ottoman's favorite vase was smashed, on top of her desk, and a pool of water and a wilting pink rose were lying beside it. She would feel very bad about that. Her brother had sent her that vase from Japan about twenty years ago. He was dead now.

Miss Claridge's desk looked all right from the front, but when you got in back of it you saw that someone had forced all her neat little drawers open and poured the stamp-pad ink over everything in them.

I sat down. It was just so sad, I could hardly bear it. One minute, I was mad enough to kill those kids, but the next, I wanted to cry. And under everything, I kept wondering—had I caused all this? Did I lock the door? It seemed to me that I had. It really did. We'd been doing this Wednesday-night bit for a couple of weeks now, and not once, not one time, even when Mr. T. had had Danish waiting for me at the restaurant, had Miss Claridge found the office door unlocked when she came to open up on Thursday morning.

The policeman left. My father came over to where I was sitting.

"Where are the typewriters, Dad?"

"Down at the station. Not that we could use them now, anyway. The boys dropped them, in an effort to get away faster, and they appear to be in pretty bad shape."

"The copier . . ."

"I saw it." He sat down on the desk, heavily, as if he felt terribly tired.

"I'm so sorry, Dad. I'll help you clean up. Free. I'll come in Saturday even."

"Thank you, Billy. Unfortunately, it'll take more than cleaning up to fix this. They've done a good deal of damage, haven't they?"

"I did lock the door."

"Billy—look at the door."

I went over and looked at it. It looked just like it always did. No different. "I don't see anything. What am I supposed to be looking for?"

"That's just it, sweetheart. There's no sign that it was forced." He sounded so sad.

"Maybe they had a skeleton key."

"I don't think so. This is a special lock. I paid extra to have it installed several months ago, when there was an epidemic of burglaries around here."

"Maybe they had a key that fit."

"Just happened to have it on them, Billy? And just happened to try it? It's possible, but it isn't probable."

Well, I know when I'm licked. If I were Dad, I would find it hard to believe that the door was locked—particularly if I were dealing with a person

101

who had lied about where she spent her afternoons, who had sabotaged a Steinway and Mrs. Ramsbottom, who met people secretly in drugstores, and who put rocks in a supply closet, causing a broken foot. Also a person with a killer sweet tooth, who loved Danish. Things did not look good for me. As a matter of fact, I wasn't sure that *I* believed in me any longer. So why should I expect my father to believe in me?

I think I would even have given up my trumpet, right then, just to have someone say, "Billy Boone, you are not responsible for all this. You did close and lock that door."

No one said it.

We went on down to the station. The typewriters rattled when my father turned them over to identify them. Oh, boy. My father had to sign some papers. Then he had to go into another office, where they were holding the kids who'd done all the damage. I waited outside. I was just relieved that they didn't put you in jail for forgetting to shut and lock a door.

When my father came out, he said, "Let's go home, Billy." That's all. And he looked stern. Very stern.

When we were in the car, I said, "Did those boys say any more about the door?"

"Yes. They repeated their earlier statement. The door was ajar—and, of course, unlocked. They noticed it and went in, on an impulse."

"Oh."

I didn't feel hungry. Neither did my father. Ma had saved plenty for us, but neither of us could eat.

After we'd sat at the table and shoved the food around for a while, my father said, "You'd better run off to bed now, Billy."

"Dad—I really thought I locked that door."

He shook his head. "Billy—"

My mother said, "It's all over and done with."

"But it isn't over. There's all that mess to clean up, and the broken typewriters . . ."

"Some of that will be covered by insurance," my father said.

"And my trumpet."

They looked at each other.

My mother said, "We can talk about that to-morrow."

They'd already decided. I could see it in their faces. I was through, as far as my job went . . . maybe as far as the trumpet went. They just didn't feel up to a big scene this late in the evening, when we were all so tired.

"Just tell me one thing, Dad. Am I still working for you or not?"

"Billy, honey, it's as much my fault as it was yours. I simply gave you too much responsibility, that's all."

"No you didn't. I did a good job at your office, didn't I? And I'm pretty sure that I locked that door."

Ma said, "Pretty sure?"

"Well, I was 100 percent sure, but now, I'm still sure—but I know it doesn't look as though I did."

Cornelia walked in. "Come on, Billy, you wouldn't admit it even if you knew you hadn't."

"You take that back. I would so admit it."

"No you wouldn't. You'd do anything to keep that trumpet going, and everyone knows it. If I were in the spot you're in, I might lie, too."

Boy, that *did* it! I was halfway around the table and moving fast before my father grabbed me. Another second or two, and I could have had Cornelia down on that rug, and I'd have turned her every which way but loose. She had no right to say that. She thinks she's such hot stuff! I happen to know she puts eye makeup on in the girls' bathroom at school every morning and takes it off every afternoon before she gets on the bus. When I see her during the day, she looks like a raccoon. And if that isn't lying—fooling Ma into thinking she doesn't use eye makeup when she does—what is?

My father held on to me while I got it out of my system. He could hold down King Kong. When I was all through, he said, "Billy, go to bed. Tomorrow's another day."

I went. When your own family doesn't trust you anymore, you're better off by yourself.

11

I just plain cut school Thursday, for the very first time in my life. I started out as if I were going to wait for the bus at the stop, but once I was out of sight, I took off for Dixie's.

She and Beagle were having their coffee in the kitchen. Dixie has hers in a mug, at the table. Beagle has his in a soup bowl, on the floor.

I told her everything . . . starting with my coming in for work at three-thirty Wednesday afternoon. The nice thing about telling Dixie anything is that she pays attention. She listens and she watches you, and every so often she'll say "Lord, have mercy!" or "You don't mean it!" or "You poor lamb"—whatever's appropriate. And you feel that you're really getting through to her.

When I finished up with playing hooky, she said,

"You poor lamb," which made me feel a lot better, and then she said, "How about a cup of coffee?"

I take mine with about an inch of cream and three sugars. And a doughnut, if it's available.

"What'll I do, Dixie? They're going to tell me I can't work at Dad's office anymore. They may even say 'no more trumpet.'"

"I don't think your father would do that, hon. Stop the trumpet, I mean. After you've done so well."

"My mother would. She hardly spoke to me last night. This morning, I didn't give her a chance. I just had juice and left."

Dixie nodded. "It's not a bad idea to let things simmer down. Sometimes people get so they see things differently after a while."

"The awful thing is, I'm not absolutely sure I did lock that door. If I could only be sure. I was sure at first, but now . . ."

"Billy, I'd bet six months of *TV Guide* that you did. Those goomers are lying."

"Why?"

"I don't know. But people who would trespass and vandalize and steal aren't going to draw the line at lying, are they?"

I sat there and gave that a little thought. If they were lying . . . and why couldn't they be? Why should everybody—even me—assume that I was the one who was lying? They were the criminals, for Pete's sake. But if they were lying, why were they?

Okay, if I couldn't figure *that* out, maybe I could figure out how they got in there without forcing the door. Okay, if I couldn't figure that out, maybe I could . . .

Dixie said, "Another dry well?"

"I don't even know where to start."

She got up and started to clear. "I've got a phone call to make, hon. You stay here and work on the Case of the Unlocked Door."

I got out my notebook and made some notes.

1. They got in without forcing the door.

2. So they had a key, or someone let them in.

3. Who would let them in? Mrs. Ottoman? She's forty-five and wears her hair braided in a coronet, and raises roses. Miss Claridge? She lives with her mother and she's taking night courses to become a lawyer. The girl who used to work there? She moved away . . . far away. Dad? Don't be silly. But no one else would have a key or access to the office.

4. If no one let them in, and they didn't have a key, maybe they got in through a window. No. The windows are all nailed shut. The whole Arcade is air-conditioned in hot weather, centrally heated in winter. If anyone had forced a window, it would have been easy to see. The police would have spotted it.

5. Maybe they came in and hid in the office till I locked up. Don't be crazy. Where would

107

they hide? The john? It's hard to fit an extra roll of toilet paper in there. Besides, I cleaned the john. Under a desk? Whose? All the desks were being used. My father left at four, but I sat behind his desk for a few minutes after that, when I was straightening it up.

Dixie came back in.
"I did leave the door open."
"It just came to you?"
"No. But nothing else fits."
"Billy, take away all the evidence, forget everything that everyone else has said, calm down, and just look into your own self. Now—take your time. Did you shut that door and lock it?"

I closed my eyes and sat there, trying to work my way back to Wednesday afternoon. I could see the office—the windows, the desk, the fading light coming through the glass roof of The Arcade and the glow of Miss Claridge's desk lamp . . . the smell of furniture polish, and the faint roar of traffic outside as the people in the city filled the streets, heading home. And then I was at the door, and I looked around the office one more time, to make sure I had turned out all the lights, and I closed that door . . . and I locked it! I could see the big brass key in my hand and feel the resistance as the key turned in the lock. "I did lock it, Dixie. I can see myself locking it."

108

"Okay. Then they were let in—which is unlikely—or they had a key."

"Yes."

"Your father says those kids are still sticking to their story, so we're not going to get any help from them."

"They were chased, and they dropped the typewriters, and the policeman got them about half a block away. They had no keys on them."

"Maybe they stuck in a typewriter."

"Well, the typewriters do rattle now, but Dad says that's because they're all banged up inside. And if they dropped the key into a typewriter, wouldn't the typewriter repairman find it?"

"*If* your father had them repaired. If they really hit the pavement hard, he might as well take the insurance money and get new ones . . . and junk these."

"Maybe they counted on that, Dixie. Maybe they threw them down extra hard, on purpose. But why wouldn't they admit it, if they had a key?"

"For one thing, having a key means premeditation, Billy, but just noticing an open door and walking in—why, that's the act of a sweet, impulsive child . . . and that calls for a lighter sentence. And there may be other considerations. Like who gave them a key, in the first place."

"Oh."

"So—what do they care if it gets you in hot water?"

"Oh."

We sat there and stared at Beagle for a while, thinking, till Beagle got nervous and got up and left.

I said, "I think we should go down there and look for a key."

"Right. You look for a key, and I'll try to get a look at those typewriters."

"What'll we do if we don't find a key?"

"Lord, Lord. I don't know."

Mr. Taglione was surprised to see me at ten in the morning.

"Hey, Billy! What are you doing—playing hooky?"

"Please, Mr. Taglione—not so loud."

He came over and whispered so you could only hear it six stools away. "You really are playing hooky? A nice girl like you?"

"Yes. I've got to see if I can find a key. Someone broke into my father's office last night, you know."

"I know. The police—they were down here at seven this morning, asking me questions."

"Dad thinks—my whole family thinks—I didn't lock up right."

"Oh, Billy. You're in a lot of trouble."

"Don't I know it! But I did. So—they had to have a key. Right?"

"Right!"

"So I'm going to find it. I figured I'd start out in

110

the street, where they caught them, before the street cleaners come along. You didn't find a key, did you?"

"No. But I'll keep my eyes open." He paused and bent down again. "Hey, Billy! Didn't the police look for a key already?"

"I guess so. But they didn't have the whole world thinking they were lying."

He gave me a fresh Danish, which I did *not* want—I will never eat another Danish as long as I live—and I started looking.

I had a lot of company. A couple of times, a dog came along and stopped and hunted with me— maybe thinking I would come up with a hamburger or something. There were a bunch of pigeons wad-dling along in the gutter, cooing at me and getting in my way until I shooed them. A policeman wanted to know what I'd lost. When I told him about the break-in, he was very sympathetic, but he went right back to directing traffic. Honestly—as if driv-ers couldn't direct themselves for a while, and let him work on something important like my father's burglary. And two little kids—both smart-mouthed little boys, also playing hooky—came along and kept pestering me with questions.

By lunchtime, I'd found a quarter, two dimes, a ballpoint pen, and a kid's wristwatch (not working). My back ached so badly I was afraid to straighten up in case it hurt worse. Dixie came up behind me. "Hi! How's it coming?"

I held out my hand and showed her what I'd found.

"You sit down, and I'll look for a while."

So I sat on the curb, beside a parking meter, and Dixie looked.

By one o'clock we were both sitting on the curb, right in front of The Arcade, in a no-parking zone.

"We'll never find it," I said.

"Maybe not. But remember—if we do, it'll prove you were not to blame."

I thought about that and decided it was worth a permanent back injury. So what if I went around for the rest of my life looking like the hunchback of Notre Dame? At least people would trust me and believe me again. I got up—and it wasn't easy!—and went over the sidewalk in front of The Arcade, square by square. Then we moved inside.

"They came down the stairs and out this door—so if it's not in this end of the walk-through, it has to be on the stairs, or somewhere up there, on the gallery, between the stairs and Dad's office."

Dixie nodded and winced. "Right."

We divided that end of the lobby in half and went over it with our noses about an inch off the floor. Then we worked our way up the stairs, which was awkward because we were sort of working against the tide of people coming down. We were almost to the top when I saw a pair of shiny brown, wing-tip shoes, size thirteen, about a foot ahead of me. Dad.

"Hey, Dad."

"Billy."

"I thought I would just skip school today and find that key for you."

"Your grandmother called me earlier. We'll discuss the skipping school later, at home. I didn't know you two planned to play Sherlock Holmes on the Arcade stairs, though."

Dixie said, "Are you going to just stand there, Charles, or are you going to help us?"

He said, "Ma—what's the point of all this?"

"Then just get back to your office. And I don't ever want to hear you argue against convicting someone on purely circumstantial evidence again— because that's what you're doing with your own daughter."

"Ma . . ."

"You've tried and convicted Billy in your mind. Some lawyer you turned out to be."

"Mother . . ." He was really getting upset, and I could see why. We were beginning to attract attention. A small crowd was gathering.

I grabbed Dixie's arm. "Gran'ma, please. Let's just you and me keep looking."

She nodded. She gave Dad one more look and bent back down to her side of the stairs. The crowd sort of flowed on down around us, and Dad went back into his office.

By three, we had covered every inch of the gallery, stairs, and lobby. Nothing. Well, no keys. We had found matches, a tiny pencil sharpener, some pennies, and a barrette. Whoever was supposed to keep those stairs clean—James or Mr. Hennessey—wasn't doing such a hot job.

We went down to Mr. Taglione's and ordered coffee and grinders.

"They'll be watching the marching band right now—the ones Mr. Kruger selected. It'll be the first time. I think he was going to let me go, too."

"You'll make it next time, Billy."

"Maybe. Maybe not. If Ma thinks I left that door unlocked, and then deliberately lied about it later, I don't know."

The sandwiches came, and Mr. Taglione refused to take any money for them. He just shook his big, grizzly head and said, "Hey—what's a friend for, eh?"

"Thanks for trying, anyway, Dixie."

"Hey—what's a friend for, eh?"

I smiled. I didn't have any laughs left in me.

Dixie went home. If Beagle's left alone too long, he gets morose and starts taking it out on the furniture. I figured I'd go home with my father.

I went up to the office and did some tidying up. Miss Claridge was still trying to clean out her drawers. Mrs. Ottoman had done a lot already. She looked real tired. I noticed that the rose and every bit of her vase were gone. It was hard for me to look at either of them. I felt guilty in that office, as if secretly they were all blaming me.

Finally, I gave up and went out onto the gallery

to wait for Dad. No one walking along the gallery cared who I was—or what I had done or not done.

I remembered the day William had leaned over the railing to throw a penny into the fountain. He'd been standing right where I was standing, and I'd grabbed him just before my father had yelled. Thank goodness! It was bad enough having my father's foot broken. If William had landed on his head in the gravel down there—or in the fountain—it would have been terrible! I did do some things right, didn't I? Then I remembered that my father yelled because a rock had fallen on his foot—one of *my* paper-weights. Honestly, I *ought* to be locked up some-where.

The fountain basin was painted a pale greeny blue, and the fountain was made of white marble. It was really pretty, and it sounded nice, too, splashing away all the time. It made you feel as if you were in a garden in the country instead of in the middle of a dirty, grimy city. Lots of people threw pennies and dimes into the fountain, for good luck. Once a month, the janitors drained it and cleaned it and sent the pennies to the United Fund. So it *was* lucky—for someone.

Then it came to me. A key is metal—just like pen-nies and dimes. Who would notice a key under the surface of the water, under all that splashing, partic-ularly with the coins scattered all around it? No one. It could lie there for weeks, till Mr. Hennessey and

James Bowden stopped the fountain late one evening to clean it.

I ran down the stairs and raced along the strip to the fountain. I didn't even remember to take off my shoes. I just hopped in and started feeling around on the bottom of the fountain with my hands. Boy! That water was cold.

People started to collect. Just any little thing will draw a crowd in our city. One man said, "Hey, sister—you're not supposed to do that."

I said, "I'm looking for something."

A kid said, "Can I look?" and I said, "Put one finger in this water and I'll break your arm."

Mr. Taglione must have heard the disturbance because he came out.

"Hey, Billy! What you doing?"

"Looking for that key."

Well, he knew what to do, right away. "All right—stand back there. Give the little girl some room. Move back."

My father came out onto the gallery over my head. I heard him clearing his throat, like he does in the courtroom.

"Billy Boone, what in the world are you doing now?"

"Looking for the key, Dad."

He started down the stairs. Luckily, it would take him a little longer than it would most people, because his foot still hurt him on stairs. Lord, if he stopped me, I might never find it. Someone else might find it. I stretched my hands out wider than I ever did for Mrs. Ramsbottom and kept going over the bottom. A couple of times I thought I had it, but it was a penny standing on edge, or a nickel.

"Billy! Get out of there this minute." My father had arrived, and was he ever mad!

"Give me another minute, Dad, please."

People in the crowd were giggling and snickering. Only Mr. Taglione seemed to feel I should keep on going.

Then, right between my own two feet, I found it! Right underneath me. A big, brass key. Just like the one my father had.

I picked it up by the tip of the skinny end. "I got it, Dad."

"Let me see."

"No. Fingerprints."

Mr. Taglione held out his clean, folded hand-kerchief, and I dropped the key onto that. He held it up very carefully and went back into the restaurant with it. "I'll get a box, Billy. You get out and dry yourself."

My dad helped me out of the fountain. I stood there dripping wet and shivering so that my teeth chattered. "I did lock the door."

"You certainly did."

"Oh, boy. Am I glad!"

He shook his head. "Billy, honey, will you please forgive me? I should have been slower to convict

117

you. I would have given any one of my clients more benefit of the doubt than I gave my own little girl."

"Does this mean I get my job back?"

"It surely does. I would be proud to have you perform my janitorial duties."

I hugged him. What's a little water on a wash-and-dry suit? Then I went into the restaurant to get the key from Mr. Taglione. He had it in a box paper napkins had come in. I hugged him, and he hugged me. Then Dad and I went to the station to give the key to the police.

Well, when the detective in charge of the case walked in and said to the kids in custody, "Guess what we found in a fountain. . . ." and flashed the key in front of them, it took them about thirty seconds to decide to put the blame on James. Good old James Bowden. To hear them tell it, James practically forced them to do his dirty work for him. And that's how they're going to build their defense in court.

James had had a duplicate made when he was still working for my father, and he had given it to them and told them to pay Dad back for firing him and to bring back something he could fence, to make it all profitable. Actually, when the police caught up with James, they found he had a large collection of office keys. I guess he had developed a sideline of theft and fencing to make his janitorial work pay more.

Because of Mr. Taglione's offers of Danish pastry,

right out loud like that, in the restaurant, everyone in The Arcade knew that I stayed late and locked up on Wednesdays . . . so the kids picked Wednesday and figured I would be their patsy.

They had tossed the key into the fountain as they left my father's office. By five-thirty, hardly anyone is left in The Arcade except for Mr. Taglione and his helpers. All James had to do was drain the fountain late some evening and pick up his key.

Tomorrow is the Fourth of July. The weather is supposed to be clear and hot—great for a parade, right? And Mr. Kruger has said I may march in the trumpet section if I limit myself to fanfares. I know he's letting me do this because a lot of the regular kids are away. That's all right. And Dixie will be there on the sidewalk, in our usual spot, to watch me march by, and Ma and Dad said they would come, too.

Ma and Dixie aren't exactly best friends, but somehow, the fact that only Dixie knew I was telling the truth about locking that door changed things at home. I can go down to Dixie's any time now, and Ma has her up once a week for dinner. Beagle comes, too—but he has to stay in the kitchen while we eat. And it is sort of understood that from now on, Dixie and I will tell the truth, the whole truth, and nothing but the truth—so help us, Robert E. Lee.